Another scream floated down the stairwell, and Rammel spun out the doorway and up the staircase . . .

Donna and Melissa, their clothes all but torn off them, cowered back on the bed, eyes wide with horror. The fat little Mex, Vargas, held a revolver on them and had just dropped his pants to his ankles, revealing a suit of red-flannel underwear. Attempting to kick free of the binding trousers, he twisted about and fired wildly. Ram felt the hot blinding concussion that blew the hat off his fair head, and shifted so that he wouldn't be firing toward the women. He squeezed the trigger.

EL PASO DEL NORTE

A Novel of the Old West

ROE
RICHMOND

ACE CHARTER BOOKS, NEW YORK

EL PASO DEL NORTE
Copyright © 1982 by Roe Richmond

An Ace Charter Original

Published by arrangement with the author.

ISBN: 0-441-20366-3

First Ace Charter Printing: October 1982
Published simultaneously in Canada

Manufactured in the United States of America

Ace Books, 200 Madison Avenue, New York, New York 10016

For:

Bob David
Mac Otis
Norry Johnson
Karl Giller
Dick Norris   } Univ. of Michigan
John Wopat
Jack McNiff
Bill Caley
Harley McNeal

Everett Coller   (Dean Academy)

EL PASO
DEL NORTE

ONE

The winter sky lowered and blackened in mid-afternoon, and the three riders bent their heads into the sleeting rain, whipped down the Rio Grande Valley by an icy north wind. The river was blotted from view, and they had long since ceased trying to watch the horsemen on the Mexican side, whose northward course paralleled their own. Suspected smugglers.

"They ain't goin to cross," Rusty Bouchard shouted through his dripping beard. "They never meant to cross, the sonsabitches."

"Not very likely," Fox Edley yelled back. "Not in this stuff."

"It's turning to snow." Milt Travers adjusted his wet scarf to cover his freezing nose and ears, shivering under his poncho and jacket.

Abruptly the world was obscured by a blinding white blizzard, and the broncs snorted and shied in protest, hooves slipping in the muck and water.

"Where's that goddamn dugout a yours, Foxface?" griped Bouchard.

Edley kneed his blue roan into line at the point. "It

1

ain't far now." Fox was the one who had remembered the dugout, built into the elbow of a ridge screened by trees, brush, and boulders, a sanctuary they badly needed. The rain had been torment enough. The snow made travel virtually impossible. Edley had fixed the landmarks in mind, before the driven snow wiped out everything.

"You're a genius, Foxcroft," said Milt Travers.

"I wintered enough up in Montana and Wyoming and Colorado," the Fox admitted modestly. "You don't forget sheltered places."

Bouchard lifted his snow-clotted bandanna and spit tobacco juice. "We have some winters up in New England too, you know."

"Yeah, I know." Edley's laugh was windtorn. "But you ain't out ridin range and campin in 'em, Red Bush. You're swillin hot rum by the fire."

"You're right, Fox." Travers booted his coyote dun forward. "Give our guide his due, Red Bush."

Bouchard grunted. "I'll give him my last jug a whisky if he gets us into shelter, Trav." In winter garb Red bulked massive on his mottled gray.

In the lee of the ridge visibility cleared a bit, and Edley led them toward his objective. They were all cloaked in clinging white.

"This gray a mine's gettin old," Bouchard grumbled. "Damn near founderin now." He yanked the horse's drooping head up.

Fox Edley laughed into the snow. "No wonder, for chrisake. He's carryin close to three hundred pounds between you and your gear."

Bouchard stiffened indignantly. "I weigh exactly two-ten, with my clothes on, Foxhead."

"On some grain dealer's crooked scales," amended Edley. "You boys take care a the hosses and I'll get a fire goin and cook supper."

The old dugout was still solid and secure; it was buried deep in the ridge, topped with a thick sod roof reinforced by timbers, and faced with tight-set logs. In the adjacent lean-to shed they stripped off saddles and gear, bundling them into the hut, and removed bits and bridles. After watering the broncs from their hats, they hung on nosebags of oats. The Fox went inside to scrounge up a fire, while Travers and Bouchard rubbed down the mounts, cleaned mudlumped shoes, and draped them with saddle blankets.

In the woodbox by the rusty iron stove, Fox Edley found enough dry paper, twigs, kindling, and buffalo or cow chips to start a fire, and the warmth spread like a blessed benediction, thawing and soothing their cold-cramped limbs and joints. Edley broke up an empty crate to add to the flames, and glanced pointedly at the empty woodbox. Bouchard and Travers sighed and plunged outside to gather more wood for drying and future fuel. The aged firebox threw intense heat, and the Rangers basked in it with luxurious pleasure as they shed wet outer garments and settled down in the flickering light of coal-oil lanterns and candle stubs. The storm howled and raged on outside, increasing their sense of comfort and well-being. They toasted the Fox with tin cups of whisky.

Fox Edley threw together a meal of beans, bacon, salt pork, biscuits, and canned tomatoes, and was spared the usual sarcastic complaints. Even the coffee tasted good when liberally laced with Travers's brandy. They utilized their own military messkits for eating and drinking.

There were four cowhide bunks against the walls, and the plank table was surrounded by kegs and halved-barrels serving as chairs. The stovepipe leaked smoke but nobody minded much. The feast finished, they washed their utensils with snow, and Travers produced a pack of long slim cigars. This is better than any Beacon Hill drawing-room, Trav reflected, and then wondered if he was striving to convince himself. He'd had doubts since he received that letter from Priscilla Cabot in Boston.

There had been little talking on the trail today. The weather was not conducive to conversation, of course, but there were deeper reasons for the undue silence. Each man had been jarred by some significant flash from his past life. It was odd indeed that these flashes had come simultaneously: Trav's scented blue envelope had no connection with the mission at hand, but Fox soon made it plain that *his* earlier experience was directly involved with the present assignment, which was riding to the aid of beleaguered Ranger Captain Rube Caldwell, in charge of the El Paso office and area.

"Susan Hope Caldwell," pronounced Fox Edley solemnly, and for once the yellow eyes were not dancing merrily in his tough lean face. "The closest I ever come to boggin down into holy matrimony. The only time I was ever ready to take that long jump in the dark."

His comrades stared in astonishment. "The woman Rube's married to, Fox?" muttered Bouchard, his wide brawny bulk rearing erect on the bunk. "You never told nobody, goddamn it."

"It ain't a thing I talk about." Edley's scarred features were mournful. "Until now I figger you oughta know. We'll be workin with Rube Caldwell."

"You and Rube still friends?" asked Travers, blue eyes frowning through the cigar smoke that wreathed his dusky blond head.

"Yeah, still friends—kinda. On a hair-trigger basis. We was like brothers once."

Travers nodded sadly. "I remember. You worked out

4

of El Paso together. You were the quick gun, Fox, and Rube was steady, the balance-wheel."

That was before Bouchard joined up, but he knew Caldwell. "Rube could tear you apart, Fox. He's a powerhouse."

"With his hands maybe. Couldn't touch me with a gun. Fast, strong, but he never had the killer instinct. Somethin a Ranger's gotta have. I don't know how Rube's lasted this long. I saved his life a dozen times. He was always holdin back, waitin to give the other guy first shot."

"He was like that," Travers agreed. "I tried to change him, but he was set solid. Nobody changed Rube Caldwell much."

Edley chewed on his cheroot. "He was crazy to take that job. Nobody else wanted it. A Ranger in El Paso ain't gotta chance, with Juarez right across the river and New Mexico just north. The local and county law won't give him no help. Outlaws pass them borders like they ain't there. It's just goddamn hopeless. But Rube wanted that promotion and extra pay for Susan and the kids. Yeah, they got three kids now."

Bouchard studied him with mild brown eyes. "You still totin a torch, Fox?"

"Hell no, nothin like that," Fox Edley said. "When she picked Rube, that was the end of it—for me." He smiled brightly. "Good thing she was smart enough to pick Rube, huh?"

Bouchard inclined his russet head with emphasis. "Christ, yes! You'd make a worse husband than me, Fox."

"You did all right with Singing Bird up in the Nations," reminded Milton Travers III, relaxed in easy grace on his barrelhead.

"That was different. She was an Injun, an Osage,

didn't want nothin or expect nothin. Just to wait on me, do things for me. Cook and keep the house clean, walk in the hills and make love." Bouchard sighed, long and wistful. "Finest gal I ever knew—anywhere. I couldn't make it with a white woman. They want too much, they wanta be boss." He shuddered and took a big drink from his cup. "White bitches castrate a man."

"And the Apaches killed her," Edley mumbled, shaking his lean dark head.

"Yeah, and I killed all of them I could run down," Bouchard said. "But it didn't help or do any good. Not really. She was gone." He relit his cigar. "Funny thing. I always heard a subchief called Quadah led that party. Never could catch up with the sonofabitch. Just the other day I got it all straight—and for sure. Quadah did lead that bunch, and it was Quadah himself who—who did it. Who raped and murdered her." Bouchard's voice broke off, and he lowered his red-bearded face into huge knotted hands.

"Is he still living, this Quadah?" inquired Milt Travers gently, after a long silence.

The red head rocked up and down, slowly.

"You still want him?"

"Not as much as I used to," Bouchard said quietly. "But I reckon I'll take him—when the time comes."

"Any idea where the bastard is?" asked Fox Edley, tasting his whisky.

Bouchard smiled bleakly in his beard. "We may be headin right for him. They say he's runnin with Cano's crew outa Juarez. And Hook Cano's s'posed to be behind all that trouble in El Paso, ain't he?"

"Christ, yes!" Edley said. "That's what Cactus Bill McKenna figgered."

Travers turned his fair head from side to side in wonder. "This is a fateful expedition. I wondered why you two guys weren't talking on the road. I *knew* why I wasn't saying much, but it had nothing to do with this job."

"Yeah, we saw that sweet-smellin blue letter from Boston, Trav," confessed Fox Edley. "And it sure shut your mouth tighter'n a clam. Was it all that bad, son?"

"I don't know," Milt Travers murmured, his finely cut face revealing no emotion. "It was an ultimatum, you might say. And I never took kindly to ultimatums."

"True confession time, Trav." Bouchard refilled his cup. "We been tellin all. It's your turn, Milton the Third."

"This girl back home, you've seen her picture—Priscilla Cabot." Travers still didn't feel like talking about it, but these two men—next to Lashtrow and Rammel—were the nearest and dearest friends he had.

"A lovely critter," Edley said, with feeling.

" 'An apparition of delight,' " quoted Bouchard gravely.

"She's been waiting all these years for me to come home and marry her."

"Damn near as long as Karen Lindley's been waitin for Lashtrow," said Edley, shifting his supple wiry shape on the kegtop.

Travers nodded. "The cases are quite similar."

"And she says the time has come. It's now—or never," Bouchard said.

"That's about it."

"Well, what are yuh goin to do, Trav?" demanded Fox Edley.

"I don't know—yet," Travers said unhappily. "I just don't know."

He could still see the lines in Priscilla's elegant flowing script:

". . . . The perfect time to break away, change your life and mine, become the man you were destined to

be. Your novel MEN AND GUNS *has suddenly become a great success, sweeping the States and selling well abroad. Your brother Kendrick went to New York and got the big critics interested. Now you are the literary man of the hour.*

You must give up Rangering before you are shot and killed. What a horrible waste that would be! Come home, settle down to a career of fulltime writing, marry me (am I not shameless?), and we can travel, live anywhere we choose, use your brilliant talents. You will become the premier literary figure of our time, darling, and the entire world will be at our feet.

Think of the joy and happiness we can share, the beauty and wonder we shall know, the glorious radiance we will walk in, the lovely children we'll raise. . . .

This is the last time I'll ask you, plead with you, humble myself to beg your favor. It has to be now or not at all, not ever . . . . They always said we were the handsomest couple in Boston. We can be the most beautiful couple in the world.

Please don't fail me again. My life as well as my love is at stake here. I cannot live without you. . . . I'll die. . . . But before God, this is my last request. Come to me now, Milton, or you'll never see me again."

"I wonder how Lash is doin up in New Mexico?" mused Rusty Bouchard. "Hope the old Wolf don't get caught in a storm like this up in them mountains. The Sacramentos can be a bitch in wintertime."

"Wonder if McKenna let Rammel go with him?" queried Edley.

"Think he did. Tess got after Bill again, and old Cactus can't say no to Tess Hiller Rammel."

Edley scowled, slitting his amber gaze. "They'll have trouble one day, Lash and Ram. God forbid it. Ram'll never forgive Lash for lovin Tess before he came along. It eats on Ram. It'll drive him to call Lash sometime."

"I doubt it, Fox. They like each other too much." Bouchard grinned at Travers, just coming out of his melancholy reverie. "Well, Trav, did you reach a decision?" He was like a kindly uncle.

"Yeah, I decided to have another drink," Travers said, with his sweet smile.

"Good thinkin, boy." Bouchard turned to Edley. "I s'pose this Susan Caldwell's a ravin beauty, too?"

"She was that. Course I dunno what she's like now, after all the years and three children. But it wasn't so much her looks. It was her whole personality, her smile and laugh, the way she thought and spoke. Charm and warmth, natural as a kitten, Susan lit up the world.

"There was a big dance out at Essling's spread. Owned a big ranch then, now he's mayor of El Paso. Rube and me got slicked up and rode out there. First time we laid eyes on Susan Hope. I never saw nothin else, resta the night. She went for me first, there was a bit of the devil in her, too. Then Rube Caldwell horned in, calm, quiet, sure and solid. About a month later I was back shootin pool, playing poker, leanin on bars, and chasin calico queens down the line. Susie saw that I was a wild bronc, too tough to housebreak, and set her cap for Rube." Edley shrugged and spread his rope-scarred palms. "I was no competition for a man like Rube Caldwell."

"Ever fight over her?" Bouchard wanted to know.

"Not really," said the Fox. "He hit me once, a cheap sucker punch, busted my nose for the seventeenth time. I wouldn't draw on him. Too easy, like burnin down a punk kid. Woulda killed anybody else, but I couldn't pull on big Rube."

"Didn't exactly break your heart, losin her?"

"Not hardly." Fox grinned. "Had some bad days and worse nights, but in the end I was glad enough to be free, I reckon."

Bouchard chortled. "You'll be nervous meetin her again, won't you?"

"Pretty goddamn likely," Fox Edley said, in disgust. "I'm human, ain't I, for chrisake?"

"There are various and conflictin opinions on that, Foxface." Bouchard's immense shoulders shook with laughter.

Edley's yellow eyes flared coldly. "You shoulda stayed a hermit, Red Bush. You got the perfect disposition for it, you hairy bastard."

TWO

It got so bad that Rube Caldwell dreaded going to the Ranger office in an adobe-brick building in El Paso. Every morning there were reports of new atrocities perpetrated by Mexican bandits against American citizens. Located at the point of north Texas, squeezed between Old and New Mexico, El Paso was a natural focal center for outlaw activity. Predators could strike and vanish almost instantly across borderlines, beyond which the Rangers had no jurisdiction.

The blame for every crime unsolved was shunted onto the Texas Rangers, and Caldwell felt as helpless as a blind mute without arms or legs.

The Border Patrol, federal-funded and uniformed, was a bureaucracy interested only in customs and immigration matters, and inadequate to control these problems. Civil and county law under the high-handed reign of Sheriff Kriewold was purely political and futile. There was no cooperation among the agencies. The Border Patrol scorned the Rangers as half-savage badge-carrying gunfighters and killers. The Rangers in turn regarded the federal officials as petty clerks in uniform.

When the Rangers did make an arrest, young Judge Milo Bascomb invariably dismissed the culprits for lack of proper legal evidence. When the Rangers shot an offender, apprehended in the act of lawbreaking, *they* were threatened with charges of manslaughter or murder. It was ridiculous, so bizarre that outsiders rated Caldwell's reports as false and impossible, even outrageous. No place could be *that* corrupt.

Rube Caldwell had finally gotten word through to Captain Bill McKenna in Austin, and Cactus Bill was sending his five best Rangers to El Paso, to assist Rube and his three regular field men. But what could five more Rangers accomplish against the legions of evil that dominated the border hotspot? A full company wouldn't have been enough, Rube thought gloomily.

El Paso was ruled rigidly by four big moguls, backed by civic law: Mayor Amos Essling, Sheriff Kriewold, Judge Milo Bascomb, and Leo Fribance, owner of the copper company and smelter. There seemed to be no way of beating them, short of killing them. And anyone who shot those four popular community leaders would be termed insane, a mad-dog killer, and either torn to pieces or strung up on the nearest lamp post.

Among the enlightened, it was common knowledge that Hook Cano and his crew of Mexican and half-breed renegades were the activists behind this regime of terrorism. Rube Caldwell should have followed the initial dictum of Foxcroft Edley, Rube's old pardner: *"Know your enemy, find him, and kill him."*

That's what Fox would have done, Caldwell ruminated sourly. That's what I should have done myself, the first thing: Go straight after Hook Cano and blast him to hell. But no one ever saw Cano, it seemed. His name was everywhere, but the man himself was never seen. He might as well be a phantom, a myth, a bloody legend to frighten children into obedience. His followers were known and seen, flitting to and fro across the Rio Grande like deadly wraiths, but never Cano himself, the satanically handsome *pistolero*, who wore an iron hook where his right hand had been shot off, and was magic and lightning with a sixgun in his left hand.

Square jaws grinding his teeth, Rube Caldwell tramped up the staircase to his second-floor office in downtown El Paso. Might as well get it over, learn the worst to start another day.

I oughta resign while I got a shred of self-respect left, Rube thought. Just the way people look at me on the street is enough to shock a man into insanity. If anyone looked that way at Fox Edley, he'd get a quick faceful of bullets. *Does Susan ever wish she'd married the Fox?* Of course she does, she must. I was always too sober and serious, too slow and stolid for Susan Hope. Foxcroft could make her laugh and sing and dance. She had fun with the Fox. I'm too practical, all business—and a god-damn failure, at that. Fox was wild as a fighting hawk, but he could make a woman happy, keep her young and gay and smiling. Yes, Susan should've married Fox Edley. I wish to God she had. Then I'd be free to give it up, run away and hide—or turn my gun on myself.

His secretary raised her untidy head with that eager look, eyes bulging behind metal-rimmed spectacles, and started to read the report aloud. Rube Caldwell snatched it from her hand and stalked on into his inner office. That woman gloated too much over bad news.

The boy clerk said, "Mornin, sir," and averted his glance from the seamed granite countenance of the captain, a powerful man with overall bigness from neck to feet, features as coarsely strong as his body.

The brevity of the report didn't decrease its horror. A young white woman, unidentified as yet, had been found in the river, nude, raped and strangled. Another Reboza victim, no doubt. Two teenage white boys had been discovered dead in two widely separated *acequias,* or irrigation ditches. An Anglo store was robbed, proprietor and wife hospitalized from brutal beatings. . . . An eighty-year-old Texan was stabbed to death in an alley. . . . The words blurred under the steaming mist of Rube Caldwell's eyes.

"Where are the men?" he asked.

"They haven't checked in yet," the clerk said.

"Jesus H Christ! They didn't check in yesterday either. What the hell's going on here?" The tirade burst roaring from a mouth that seldom swore, and the clerk cringed in surprise and fear. Caldwell went on, "I got three goddamn Rangers where I need a regiment, and I can't find them three. How in the name a Jesus they expect me to operate in these conditions?"

Rube grabbed the recently-installed telephone and cranked furiously. After numerous complications and delays, he got through in turn to Sheriff Kriewold, Mayor Essling, Judge Bascomb, and Leo Fribance. None had seen or heard anything of his three Rangers. Each inquired with malice if he had learned about last night's murders and crimes. Caldwell was fairly frothing at the mouth when he finally slammed down the receiver.

This was the end. He couldn't take any more. Had to do *something.* But what? Anything, for chrisake. Anything was better than nothing. Marching to the closet, Rube replaced his derby with a slouch hat, his frock coat with a sheepskin jacket. He buckled on a shell belt with two holstered .45s, and tied down the sheath bottoms. He had always been calm, stern, controlled. Now something had snapped. He phoned the livery stable with orders to ready his black stallion.

Rube Caldwell would ride across the Rio Grande into Juarez, Mexico, find that sonofabitch Hook Cano, and shoot him dead.

14

The clerk gaped at him in wonder. "Where are you goin, sir, in case—?"

"Out," Rube snarled. "Out to kill some people. That's what a Ranger's s'posed to do, ain't it? If anyone asks, just say I'm out."

Out of my friggin mind, he thought, striding for the door. "You hold the fort, kid," he called over his wide shoulder. "There'll be five more Rangers pullin in here someday—soon."

"But, Captain Caldwell, sir, what'll I—?"

"Rest easy, son, don't fret," Rube said kindly. "It don't matter one way or another, just remember that. Don't make any difference—in the end. We live till our time comes, then we die. So it don't really matter a goddamn bit, kid. You can't win anyway. Everybody loses. Nobody wins. So don't take it too serious, boy. That was always my trouble. It's better to go laughin. So what the hell, son? It's all a joke, but we don't find out till it's too late."

Clomping down the stairs Rube Caldwell was more rational. Fox Edley would be here before long. Once the closest friend Rube ever had. He was one of McKenna's top five, naturally. Hard to picture anyone better than the Fox with a Colt, yet Lashtrow was rated number one, already a legend. Travers, the rich pretty boy from Harvard was second, impossible though that seemed. Or maybe tied for second with Bouchard, former trailtown marshal and squaw man, whom the Osages named Red Bush. Then came the Fox, and a kid from Virginia, Rammel. Rube knew them all, and kept track of them through the grapevine and official bulletins and news stories.

He'd have to invite them out to the house for supper —if he was still around. How would it go when his wife met Edley again? Susan was as pretty as ever, prettier since she'd ripened and filled out, bloomed. Rube didn't imagine Fox had aged or changed much. Fox was no beauty. Looked like what he was, ex-outlaw, bronc twister, hired gun. But he had something women liked. It'd probably go right and smooth. Susan was a lady, the mother of three, and Fox Edley was a gentleman, even if he had been born over a saloon in Rock River, Wyoming. Sure, everything would be fine as silk. Fox never held it against Rube for winning out with Susan.

But Rube Caldwell, head of the household, might not be there for the reunion. He was still determined to cross into Ciudad Juarez and hunt down Hook Cano. The possibility that his three Rangers might be dead now chilled him to the bone, but did not deter him. He was just doing what Fox Edley would have done long before. How many innocent lives would have been spared? He mourned the other Rangers who'd vanished here.

Emerging onto the board sidewalk, Rube turned toward the livery barn and bumped squarely into Lily Lavoy, her smile as bright as the morning sun that made a halo of her spun-gold hair, scarlet gown low on her magnificent bosom and molded skintight to her lushly exaggerated curves, jade eyes brilliant under long curled lashes. She clasped his biceps with frank delight, and looked up at him in open adoration.

"Howdy, Rube! Long time no see. Buy a drink for a poor lady of the streets." She wore a rich fur jacket over the scarlet dress.

"Would if I had time, Lily," said Caldwell, cheeks warm from the attention they were attracting from passing pedestrians and horsemen. "Got an important meeting at the livery stable. I'm late already, in fact."

"Surely you can spare a few minutes for an old friend and admirer, who hasn't seen you for months—that seem like years. Come on, Rube, loosen up a little. Just one quick drink together. Is that too much to ask from the man you idolize?"

"Cut it out, Lil," muttered Caldwell, cheeks and ears now burning.

"I only speak the truth from my heart."

"All right, Lil, okay." It was probably the quickest way out of this. "The Franklin Hotel bar satisfactory?"

"One of my favorite spots, among all the glittering joints that grace El Paso," declared Lily Lavoy, taking his arm and pressing close. "I can feel snow coming, Rube, and it depresses me. You must cheer me up."

Caldwell smiled ironically. "I'm in no mood to cheer anyone up, Lily."

"Uh-huh, I saw the paper this morning. The bloody bastards are still at it, aren't they?"

"You seen anything of my three boys?"

Lily considered shortly. "Not in the last few days, come to think of it. Thought you'd sent them out on some mission or other. Why are they so anxious to get rid of you Rangers?"

Caldwell laughed harshly. "Because we're the only law enforcement agency that tries to enforce the law."

"It's that bad with our hierarchy, huh? God help us all. Is it true the Big Five's coming from headquarters?"

"Word sure gets around," Caldwell said dryly. "Yeah, they're comin, Lil."

"I can't wait to see Fox Edley again, and old Red Bush Bouchard. Big Lash and that handsome Travers. Don't recall meeting any Ranger named Rammel."

"He's as good-lookin as Travers," said Caldwell. "Matter of fact, they look like brothers. Rammel's younger and blonder. How do you know about the Big Five anyway?"

Lila laughed lightly. "You pick up a lot of news items, hanging around saloons and parlor houses. I remember Rammel now. Marcia Mangan's flame."

A notorious character up and down the Rio Grande from El Paso to Laredo, Lily was a strange professional,

17

preferring to freelance rather than work for a house or cabaret. When working "from hunger," as she put it, Lily would accept any client who could pay her rather exorbitant fee. When not working she would reject the Prince of Wales and all his royal wealth, but bed down for free with a man of her choice—like Rube Caldwell. She'd waged a campaign of seduction on Rube for years, and succeeded a few times, despite his strait-laced moral code, and his devotion to wife and family.

"Maybe you know where Hook Cano hides out?" Caldwell suggested, as they entered the colorful stained-glass door at the side of the Franklin Hotel.

"Only God knows that, I guess," Lily Lavoy murmured, as they selected the discreet alcove table she favored and ordered their drinks. Lily wanted a double brandy, and Caldwell took a sherry.

"You aren't any more of a drinker than a lover, Rube," sighed Lily.

"True, very true. You know Cano's men, don't you?"

"Not intimately, I'm happy to say. But I've seen most of them around, here and there. Tatum, Fasaro, Pablito, Quadah, Chacon, they're the tophands." She shivered slightly.

"Good with guns?"

"*And* knives and hatchets. Or they wouldn't be with the Hook."

Caldwell sipped his sherry. "You've seen Cano himself?"

"Two or three times perhaps," Lily said, accepting a light for her long brown cigarette. "A great play-actor, handsome as the devil, always smiling, flourishing his steel hook of a right hand. A strutting peacock in fancy charro clothes braided with silver. Contempt in his eyes and manner, contempt for everything. A superb horseman and the fastest Mex gun since Chief Calderon and Juan Salvador."

"Salvador wasn't that fast—except with his mouth."

"Well, Calderon was. It took Lashtrow to beat *him.*"

"I know, Lily." Rube stared over her golden head with a faraway look. "I'm goin over to Juarez after Hook Cano."

"You're going out of your mind, man!" She gazed at him in disbelief. "You're crazy! You want to commit suicide, there are easier ways."

"It's the only way to stop this killin."

"Maybe so. But you can't do it alone, Rube," Lily Lavoy declared. "You're too gentle, kind, and good to be a real gunfighter, Rube. Wait'll the boys from Austin come, for the love of God!"

"I'm goin, Lil. I gotta go." Caldwell's heavy jaws were set and ridged with muscle, his lips compressed into a thin straight line under the bold blade of his nose. "I can't live with this anymore."

"Your death won't settle a goddamn thing," Lily stated flatly. "It's what they want, you big stubborn mulehead. Either dead or gone from El Paso, that's the way they want you. Why don't you resign, Rube? You were never meant to be a Ranger anyway. A Ranger has to be a killer. You're no killer, Rube."

"I'm goin to be one, by God," gritted Caldwell. "I'm crossin the river."

"I'll come with you then. They know me over there. It'll save you from getting shot down the minute you hit Mexican soil. For some reason they respect me, God knows why. Even Hook Cano won't shoot at me, Rube."

Caldwell shook his large black head. "I can't let you come, for chrisake! Hide behind your skirts. They'd laugh us outa town. That'd take away the last ounce of self-respect I got left."

"My palomino mare needs exercise. I been wanting to take her out for days now. What better than a little

19

canter across the bridge?" Lily drained her brandy goblet. "A nice young couple out for a ride before the snow comes. Your black stud looks good with my golden mare. We'll make a striking foursome. At least you'll get a chance to look around Juarez, before you get shot out of the saddle."

"No, I can't do it. It don't make sense."

"If you won't take me, I'll follow you," Lily persisted grimly. "You can't stop me from doing that, Rube. Come on, let's get our horses."

Rube Caldwell groaned. "Goddamn it, I would have to run into you this mornin. My luck never changes for the better. I can't win for losin."

Lily Lavoy laughed her full robust laugh, fairly brimming with life, energy and vital health. How could she do it, living the kinda life she did?

"It may turn out to be the best thing that ever happened to you," Lily said cheerily. "You may be thankful the rest of your days that you met me this fine winter morning in El Paso del Norte. It could be the turning point of your entire career, my big and slightly stupid friend."

"Maybe," Rube admitted grudgingly. "But I doubt it like hell."

They left the hotel barroom and walked toward the stable, the pale wintry sun shining on the rough barren heights of the Franklin Mountains, through which the Rio Grande had cut this passage and given the settlement its name. The air was blowing fresh and clean, edged with an icy sharpness and the tang of coming snow.

Rube Caldwell breathed deeply and felt a mite better. Just being with Lily renewed the life, strength and hope within him.

THREE

Up in New Mexico, over a hundred miles northeast of El Paso, Lashtrow and Rammel had been too late to save Ashley's Anvil spread. The ranch had been burned to the ground, house, barns, barracks, and sheds, the corrals and pens torn apart, a desolate fire-blackened scene. People, cattle, and horses were gone, except for a few dead animals strewn about the charred ruins. There were no human bodies or fresh graves, no clue as to exactly what had happened here. The herd, estimated at around a thousand head, had been driven off into the Sacramento Mountains toward El Paso, but what had become of the Ashley family and their crew?

It was finally decided that Lashtrow would follow the cattle drive, while Rammel went to the nearest settlement of Pinon to see if the Ashleys had taken refuge—or been buried—there. If not, Ram might discover some details of the occurrences at Anvil, before hitting the trail for El Paso, which was obviously the destination of the herd, as well as the rendezvous point for the Rangers with Captain Rube Caldwell.

Now, high in the mountain wilderness of the Sacramento Range, Lashtrow and his sorrel had been caught in a snowstorm. It had started innocently enough, the flakes large and soft and lazy, and Lash had expected to reach a cabin in a sheltered valley he knew, before the real storm broke. But he was still on the mountain trace above it when the blizzard struck with sudden fury. The cattle were on a lower more open trail.

The rustlers, not too far ahead by the previous signs, should have reached the valley, but even there they might lose half the herd in a winter storm such as this promised to be. Right now Lashtrow's prime concern was survival, and his prospects anything but bright.

Sleetlike snow, smoking and swirling, stung and blinded him, while the ripping wind beat upon his tall rangy frame and tore the breath from his lungs. Hat pulled low and bandanna drawn high over nose and ears were fragile protection against these elements. The great sorrel stayed calm and steady beneath him, but both horse and rider were soon glazed with a thickening crust of ice, smothered and buffeted by the wind-lashed snow —lost, helpless, and in danger of freezing to death, as the temperature plummeted to sub-zero depths.

Caught like the rankest greenhorn, Lashtrow thought in disgust, stupid as an ox. Head bent into the howling blast, hat tugging at his chinstrap with choking force, the big Ranger shivered inside his sheepskin-lined jacket and heavy chaps, as the intense cold knifed through him. He had been fairly close to the pass he wanted, dropping steeply down into the valley. With luck he might make it, although he could barely see the horse's head in the gusting whiteness. By instinct more than anything else, and the sorrel's more than his, Lashtrow pressed onward, the ferocity of the gale almost tearing him bodily from the saddle.

In occasional brief lulls he searched hungrily for landmarks, but the whipping snow erased them again before Lash could be certain. The pass should be in this direction. It *had* to be. Bucking the wind and hail, they plodded on, Lashtrow hunched agonizingly in the iced leather. Gradually his anguish faded into deadly warning numbness. This was no way to die, for chrisake. He'd envisioned death coming in blazes of gunfire, but not like this, not winter-killed like a stray dumb steer, dying by inches. Yet death was closing in, penetrating, spreading with the numbness.

Lash was near to despair when he glimpsed a vague blurred breach in the solid white barrier before him, on the left. The head of the pass. It must be, thank God! Once in it, skidding downward, he couldn't miss the basin and the cabin below—*if* the cabin still stood. It might be filled with bandit gunmen, but to hell with them. He'd rather go that way than this.

There was some relief in the narrow defile, and the sorrel made good time sliding down the whitened chute, thrashing out into the small mountain-rimmed bowl, where a creek had run beside a sturdy log hut. Pray to the Lord it was still there, somewhere in that dense whirlpool of snow.

In the sunken valley the violence lessened, but visibility wasn't much better. Lashtrow's ice-crusted eyes searched from one side to the other, finally picking out a dark smudge on the right. He kneed the horse in that direction. The sorrel shied suddenly, and Lash saw gratefully that they'd almost blundered into a log wall in the blind white welter of the blizzard. The cabin was there, and they'd beaten death one more time.

He got down stiffly, no more feeling left in his legs and arms, found the high broad door, shouldered it open after a struggle, and led his bronc inside. It was a vast relief to escape the outer chaos and turmoil.

The cabin was like an ice-box, but it seemed a warm haven with the savage slashing furies shut outside. There was a crude fieldstone fireplace, kindling and chunks of wood piled in a nearby corner. With numb awkward fingers Lashtrow peeled off his rigid gloves and managed to start a fire on the open hearth. Man and horse were soon steaming, as the ice and snow melted off them. Once his hands were functioning properly, Lash removed bit and bridle, saddle and gear, drank brandy from a bottle, poured canteen water into his hat for the sorrel to muzzle, then divested himself of the heavy jacket and chaps.

"Lucky again, Mate," he said, pacing about to restore circulation and limber up. "Once more the wolves miss out on us. But if we hadn't hit that pass, Soldier, we'd have been finished for sure. Frozen stiff and buried deep in the snow."

Lighting an old kerosene lamp, Lash hung a grainbag on the sorrel's head and gave him a brisk rubdown. Then he opened his saddlebags and began preparing some food for himself, nipping at the brandy now and then.

It was splendid to feel alive, warm and mobile again. The one-room cabin was spacious, fitted with rude benches and tables, packing-boxes for chairs, and built-in bunks with horsehide stretched over straw mats and rope springs. The place became surprisingly snug and homelike, as the fireplace crackled red and cheerful, the lamp flickered soft and yellow over the opened saddlebags and bedroll, and the brandy bottle gleamed on a table above the utensils from the messkit. The beef stew Lash had packed and the boiling coffee exuded delicious odors, and there was a can of pears for dessert.

Stripped down for comfort in the growing heat, Lashtrow devoured his meal washed down with brandy-spiked coffee, cleaned the dishes and implements with snow, and lounged back with a long thin cigar in his teeth to contemplate many things.

Rammel must have been trapped back in Pinon by the

storm, which would not be bad if the Ashleys were there, alive and unhurt. The lanky gaunt-faced Ashley, a Texan and friend of Bill McKenna and Rube Caldwell, was a fine man with a gracious wife Amanda and a charming daughter Donna. Ram was certain to take an interest in the vivacious young girl, married man or not. It hadn't been completely comfortable, riding the long trails with Rammel.

His thoughts turned to Rube Caldwell's precarious situation in El Paso, sometimes referred to as "Hell's Hottest Corner," located as it was on a narrow projection between Old Mexico and the Territory of New Mexico, with only the Rio Grande separating it from Ciudad Juarez.

The most vicious and ruthless of the *bandidos,* Hook Cano's gang, murdered, robbed and pillaged on both sides of the Line, striking in El Paso mainly and vanishing instantly south to their native Juarez or north into the wastes of New Mexico. When Ashley had appealed to McKenna for aid, he had inferred that the threat he feared came from Cano's outfit, which had previously driven him out of Texas.

Rube Caldwell lacked the manpower to cope with the enemy. Only three Rangers were left on his staff. Through the years others had disappeared, one by one, never to be heard from again. In Ranger ranks, being posted to El Paso was the equivalent of a death sentence. Lashtrow often marveled that Caldwell was still alive. More than once Lash had advised Rube to request a transfer, or to resign. But Big Rube Caldwell was determined and proud. However hopeless the odds, he would not quit.

Unable to spare a larger force, Cactus Bill McKenna had dispatched his famous Big Five to El Paso. Travers, Edley, and Bouchard, who'd been tracking smugglers up the Rio Grande, were to continue on to El Paso, while

Lashtrow and Rammel would return from their New Mexico project to meet them there and join up with Caldwell's decimated squad.

It was, Lash decided morbidly, the very worst mission they had ever undertaken, and all of them had been bad enough.

Savoring another tin cup of cognac, Lashtrow fancied he heard cattle bawling somewhere back in the east. The Ashley herd had kept to the lower, more open passages, and it might be that he had arrived here ahead of them. Then he reasoned that it was only the wind torrents crying through the mountain cuts and notches. But the sounds came again. Putting on hat, jacket, and gloves, Lash took a pail and lunged outside to break scum ice and dip a pailful of aching-cold water from the tiny creek. The storm had slackened a trifle, the height of its fury spent.

On the way back the wind brought, along with its own heavy roar, the unmistakable bleating bawls of cattle from the northeast end of the valley. It was the herd all right, lost, panicky, freezing, and dying out there. Lash wanted to save Ashley's stock, but he didn't care to tangle with a crew of Hook Cano's cutthroat bastards. He debated about firing a couple of shots into the air, and finally resolved it was better not to tempt fate.

They might see the log house and they might not, but Lashtrow wasn't going to call their attention to it. He checked his Winchester and Colts, laid out plenty of extra .44–40 ammunition, doused the lights, and waited in the darkness at a rifle slit. There were no real windows.

The wind and snow were letting up, the air clearing gradually except for ground-fog, and the crying of cows and steers sounded louder. The first of the cattle drifted into view like ghostly creatures in a mirage, plowing and scrambling weakly through the deep drifts. A few floundered and fell, and drovers looking like snowmen fought

26

to rouse and keep the animals moving. Then a high hooded wagon lurched out of the mist, drawn by six weary, wallowing mules. The bundled-up, snow-plastered figure on the seat resembled a woman in bearing and movements.

The black sky lifted and opened a trifle, and pale intermittent rays of moonlight filtered through. Lashtrow perceived that the driver *was* a woman, and one he recognized—Mrs. Amanda Ashley. It was incredible that the Ashleys had retained their herd, after having their ranch burned out, but that seemed to be the case. The tall man straining to lift a cow from a snowbank was Ashley himself, Lash realized, as he relit the lamp and candles, opened the door, and called out into the night:

"Hey, Anvil! Ashley! Shelter in here. Come on over."

Ashley had the cow on its feet, shoved it on forward, and turned with gun in gloved fist. "Who's there? Who the hell is it?"

"Lashtrow—from the Rangers."

Ashley put his gun away and led his horse toward the cabin, cowboys straggling after him, as Amanda whipped, reined, and turned the ponderous ice-covered wagon in that direction. Lash moved his sorrel out into the long shed beside the hut, and the riders left their broncs there, before stumbling into the warmth of the main building. Ashley helped his wife down and escorted her to the glowing entrance, both sagging with fatigue.

The cattle were strung along the creek, that crossed the valley floor, breaking the ice to drink and huddled together for warmth. Inside the cabin the newcomers were chilled, exhausted, ready to drop. Lashtrow got out a bottle of whisky and passed it around. Ashley introduced his three riders: Cobb and Mullen and Val Verde. "Where the hell's Arizona?"

"He was back with the *remuda* and the drag," the burly Cobb said. "Oughta be here by now."

"Gotta go back and get one of my men," Ashley said, gulping whisky.

"Better let me go," Lashtrow said quietly. "I'm warm and rested." He gathered his saddle, blanket, and bridle.

"I'll go with you, Ranger," said little Val Verde. "My bronc's still strong."

"Wait in here till I get saddled up." Lash went out to the shed, the cold striking through him like iced spears. The temperature had risen, but it was still frigid. The turbulence had subsided, the snow ceased.

Val Verde joined him and they rode toward the eastern end of the basin. "Arizona's my best friend," he said simply.

"How come you still got the herd after what they did to the ranch?" queried Lash.

"Beats hell, don't it? We was all out roundin up stock, and the missus had taken Donna, the daughter, into Pinon to see the doc. She'd been feelin poorly. The sonsabitches hit the spread and put torches to it. Woulda took the cattle but a cavalry troop happened by just in time, and the goddamn rustlers lit out for the hills."

"Donna stayed in Pinon?"

"Good thing, too. She wasn't fit to travel, specially in this weather. It woulda killed her sure."

They were beginning to meet steers from the drag, and horses from the *remuda*, but there was no sign of Arizona as yet.

"Christ, he'll be froze to death," Val Verde moaned.

"Not if we find him quick enough."

"I feel for the Ashleys. Lost everything they had in the world. Us boys did too, but we didn' have enough to matter. . . . Hey, there's his hoss!"

Lash saw the riderless bronc, saddle askew, reins trailing, flank gashed and bleeding through a film of ice and

28

snow. "Musta fell in the rocks," Val said. "We gotta hurry, man."

A few minutes later they came upon Arizona, lying by the trail half-buried in a drift, unconscious but alive. Frozen blood marked his head and face, but Lash didn't think he was badly injured. The worst danger was from exposure. Carefully and gently they lifted him and hoisted his inert form across the sorrel's back, in front of the pommel. "He'll be all right, Val." Lashtrow climbed on to hold him in place, and they started back. "Storm stopped in time. He's okay."

"If he ain't there's goin be a lotta dead greasers round El Paso," Val Verde said tightly, using his reata to haul a cow out of a snowbank.

"Was it Hook Cano's gang?" Arizona's paint horse limped along after them.

"Yeah, it was them. We gotta look at a few of the bastards. Pablito, Tatum, Fasaro, Quadah."

"You seen 'em since you started the drive, Val?" asked Lashtrow.

"No, but I'll guarantee they ain't far away. Either follerin or frontin us. Prob'ly woulda jumped us, if the storm hadn't broke out."

"You lose many head?" Lash kept a firm grip on Arizona's buffalo jacket.

"Not too many, considerin. Not yet anyway. Figure we got over a thousand left." Amber slits from the cabin showed invitingly ahead.

Lashtrow scowled thoughtfully. "Could be they're just letting you drive the herd to El Paso for 'em."

"Yeah, that notion occurred to me, Lash," said Val Verde somberly. "Wouldn't be a bit surprised if that's what the sonsabitches had in mind. Don't trust that Yeager, who owns the stockyard in El Paso."

Ashley came out to attend to their horses and Arizona's paint, while Lashtrow and Val Verde carried the unconscious cowboy into the hut. Cobb and Mullen were already snoring in their bedrolls on the floor, and Amanda Ashley rested on one of the bunks. Lash probed, cleansed, and sterilized Arizona's head wounds, finding no evidence of skull fracture. Val Verde wrenched off the boy's ice-stiffened clothes and gave him a vigorous and thorough massage, during which Arizona opened his eyes and grinned up at them. The eyes gave evidence of brain concussion, Lashtrow diagnosed.

"Damn-fool paint fell and I lit on my thick head. Thought I was a goner for sure."

"You're going to be fine," Lash assured him.

"If Val don't rub all my skin off."

Amanda prepared a hot plaster of mustard and flour, which was placed on Arizona's chest, and Lash fed him some quinine tablets from his first-aid kit. "What I really crave is a drink," Arizona said, and Lash gave him a cup of brandy. The young rider was soon asleep, with Val Verde watching over him. Dangerous to sleep with a head wound, but it couldn't be avoided.

Ashley returned with a bucket of water, lanky, gaunt-featured, and sad-eyed. "Arizona okay? Weather's gettin better by the minute. We're goin to save mosta the herd, Amanda."

"Well, it's all we've got left, Ash," his wife murmured.

Lash handed Ashley a cup of brandy. "What's this Hook Cano got against you folks, Ash?"

Ashley shrugged and wagged his narrow head. "He tried to court Amanda once, and she cut him dead. Cano fancies himself a lady killer, and his pride was hurt. That's the only reason I can figger, Lash."

In the firelight Lashtrow's eyes changed from gray to green. "That man's lived way too long."

"At one time it was said Cano was after Rube Caldwell's wife, too. But I doubt he got anywhere with Susan."

"I doubt it too." Lashtrow swallowed some more brandy. "You're planning to sell the herd in El Paso?"

"What else, Lash? I got no place to run 'em, no money to buy another spread. If I did set up somewhere else, it wouldn't be long before Hook Cano hit it."

"Why El Paso? That's Hook's home field."

"Huffnail and Millhauser offered me the best price," Ashley explained.

"You trust them?"

"As much as anybody in El Paso, I reckon," Ashley said, with a wry grin. "Did Cap'n McKenna send you up here by yourself, Lash?"

"No, he sent two of us. Big deal, huh?" Lash's smile was satirical. "When we found the place burnt out, Rammel went on to Pinon to find out what happened. We never figured to find you with the cattle, Ash."

"Donna's in Pinon. Rammel can bring her to El Paso, when she's well enough to travel. That's good, very good."

"Yeah, that'll work out well. A pleasure for Rammel. He's about Donna's age, a fine boy. A gentleman from Virginia." But Lashtrow didn't know if it was really good or not. They were bound to be attracted to one another, and perhaps too strongly. Of late Ram seemed more susceptible to outside women, although he had resisted the charms of Inez Carrizo in East Texas. That was no easy accomplishment for any young man, married or single. Just thinking of Inez stirred a prickle of desire in Lashtrow.

Well, it was fate and beyond Lash's control. It would be strictly between Donna Ashley and Aubrey Rammel. There were larger problems to worry about, like getting the cattle to El Paso, and holding them safely once there. The raiders would be lurking somewhere in these mountains.

FOUR

On the ride toward Pinon Rammel was in a mood of deep melancholy. It seemed a pointless trip, in the first place. The Ashleys were either dead or long gone. The fire-reeking ruins of their ranch had depressed Ram, reminding him of the Union-burned southern mansions he had seen in childhood. He felt that Lashtrow wanted to get rid of him; there had been tension between them on the long trek north. There'd always be an undercurrent of tension, now that Rammel knew the truth about Lash's intimacy with Tess Hiller before Ram came along and married her.

The air was colder, rife with the ozone smell of a coming storm, and the northern sky was low and purpling to blackness. The Virginia-bred Rammel hated the cold and snow. This was one expedition he should have sat out, much as he hated the office routine at headquarters in Austin. He missed Tess and his son, little Trav, with a hollow lonely pain under his breast-bone. The odds were so high against them in El Paso, the whole mission seemed hopeless. A handful of Rangers against an army of bandits. It was always the case, and a miracle that the Texas lawmen ever survived.

The cavalry company was double-filing out of Pinon,

32

as Rammel approached the settlement. The captain pulled out when Ram gestured, the Ranger star in his palm, and the column trotted on in its dustcloud. The captain had a ruddy, weathered countenance and a tobacco-stained gray mustache. In response to Ram's question, he said crisply:

"We were too late to save the ranch, but in time to drive off the rustlers and save the herd. The Ashleys started driving the cattle through the Sacramentos for El Paso, despite the storm threat. The renegades had at least eight or ten men, the Ashleys only five. But Ash was determined to go. Miss Ashley is at the doctor's in Pinon."

"Thank you, Captain." Rammel saluted casually, with the old VMI flair, thinking whimsically: I should've joined the Army. It's a helluva lot safer than the Rangers. In the cavalry you may even outnumber the enemy, on occasion. But he didn't like discipline, and as a trooper he wouldn't have met Milt Travers, Fox Edley, Rusty Bouchard—or Lashtrow. He still admired the hell out of Lash, and was proud of being one of the Big Five.

Rammel watched the blue-clad troopers pass, a strange admixture of leathery veterans and fresh-faced recruits, and silently wished them the best of fortune. They were far away from homes and families and sweethearts, in a great barren wilderness peopled with savages, outlaws, and animals, and forever flanked by danger and death.

Jogging on toward town, the ominous pressure of a winter storm building steadily overhead, Rammel wondered how ill Donna Ashley was. Lash had told him she was a pretty young lady, lively, flirty, wise beyond her years. If Donna were well enough to be up about and talk, it would give him something to look forward to in this isolated frontier community.

Rammel had never been a woman-chaser, although his good looks, natural grace, and charming courtesy made him attractive to the opposite sex. But he was beginning to believe that marrying so young had robbed him of many rich and glamorous experiences that should be an integral part of growing to maturity. Marriage should not emasculate a man, yet in his case it had seemed to; fatherhood only compounded the process. He had to envy his comrades who, while older than Ram by from six to a dozen years, were single and free as the wind. He felt prematurely tied down, barred from the mainstream of life.

Rammel didn't want to be unfaithful to his wife and son, whom he loved beyond words, yet neither did he want to lose out on all the excitement and pleasure a man in his twenties ought to be enjoying. Time was fleeting, and opportunities passed up were gone forever.

Travers had confided his own dilemma to Rammel, and Ram was all sympathy but reluctant to offer any advice. It was a personal predicament that no one but Travers himself could solve. Ram didn't want to lose Trav, but he realized that Priscilla Cabot was right. With all that literary talent, Trav ought to hang up his guns, go home to Boston and marry the girl, settle down to a writing career. Yet Rammel dreaded the thought of living in a world without Milton Travers III.

"I don't know what to do," Trav had admitted. "I'm getting up around thirty, a good age to marry if you're ever going to. I feel the need to write, and I've never considered marrying anyone but Priscilla. But I don't want to leave the Rangers. You and Lash, Red Bush and the Fox."

"We sure don't want you to go," Ram had answered. "But with that great gift you have, the sensible thing would be to use it, I suppose. Before you get shot in the back in some crummy border cantina. You owe it to yourself, your family, Priscilla—and the world."

"I'm not that great, Ram." Travers laughed in self-deprecation.

"You might be, Trav," said Rammel. "You have the potential. Your two books more than prove that."

"Well, we'll wait and see. This junket up in El Paso could settle it, once and for all." Trav's blue eyes had held a sad faraway look, as if he were seeing himself, and perhaps all his friends, dead under gunsmoke in some El Paso ditch.

Now, shivering inside, Rammel brought himself back to the present and surveyed the rough scatter of adobe, frame and split-log structures that formed the town of Pinon, with the usual commercial places huddled about a central square. Lamplight already blossomed in some windows, as darkness closed down early and the cold sharpened to a steel edge. The breath of the big bright bay and its rider vaporized on the frosty air, as they cantered in between hitchracks, raised board sidewalks, horse troughs, and false-fronted stores with signs creaking in the wind, under the overhangs.

The northern ramparts of the Guadalupe Mountains loomed beyond the settlement, lofty and mysterious on the eastern skyline, blurred by the encroachment of early winter night. There were few pedestrians abroad, but plenty of saddle broncs and all variety of rigs lined along the hitchrails. The Mescalero Saloon seemed to be the center of activity, and the ramshackle Otero House passed for a hotel. Set well back from the plaza was the livery barn with a blacksmith shop, sheds, and corrals. Rammel left his bay there, assured that the hostlers would take the best of care with such a fine horse, and walked out to the square, head ducked into the biting gusts, spitting grit from the dust that flayed his stubbled cheeks.

A bath and shave were first in order. Ram carried his saddlebags into the barbershop and learned it had all the facilities. The barber shaved his beard and trimmed his blond hair, while the water was heating for his bath at the rear. The barber discussed the raid on Anvil and the visit by the U.S. Cavalry. "They're never round when the goddamn Injuns come down on us outa the Guadalupes." Rammel lay back and listened.

The bath was a delightful luxury. His dirty clothes soaked in a smaller tub nearby. Rammel laid a .44 Colt on a shelf within reach, a precaution he'd acquired from Lashtrow. He owed so much to the big guy, it was a shame he couldn't forget that Lash had been Tess Hiller's first lover. Ram knew that Lash regretted it as much as he did, but it couldn't be undone or forgotten.

Dressed in a fresh outfit from his saddlebags and nipping at a bottle of brandy, Rammel felt like a new man, glowing clean, fit and strong and ready for anything.

He wrung out his washed clothing and hung it up to dry, telling the barber he'd pick it up tomorrow. "Do you know how sick Miss Ashley is?" he inquired.

The man smirked slyly. "Don't reckon she's sick at all. She and the doc got somethin goin 'tween them. He's one helluva ladies' man, Doc Keech is. He'd screw a snake if he could hold it."

"Where's she staying?"

"Right there at Keech's. He's got rooms for patients, a special room for Donna Ashley prob'ly."

"Is he a good doctor?"

The barber snorted disparagingly. "He's a christly butcher. Don't believe he's a real doctor nohow. Them diplomas he's got framed on the walls are friggin fakes. A man shot in the arm or leg goes to him, Keech'll cut off that arm or leg. Even if it's a flesh wound. You'll see a lotta one-armed and one-legged men in this town, brother."

"Sounds like a real noble character," Rammel remarked. "How come a nice girl like Donna Ashley goes for him?"

"All the damn-fool women go for the sonofabitch. It's like he hypnotizes 'em or somethin. He's got them kinda big piercin eyes, and he's a smooth-talkin bastard."

"A good-looking man?"

"Christ, no! He's ugly as a wart hog—except for them oversize eyes."

Rammel grinned and shook his fair head. "There's no accounting for the taste of women. Well, I've got to see Donna Ashley anyway."

"Keech won't let yuh in. He won't let yuh see her," the barber declared.

"How's he going to stop me?" Rammel patted the gun sheathed on his right thigh. Its twin was slung under his left armpit, in the style of Fox Edley.

"Keech's better with guns than medicine. A sneak shooter, packs a belly-gun and sleeve-gun. He's killed a few men here. Always self-defense. But the other gent never gets off a shot."

Rammel's grin was boyish. "Some doctor! Thanks for tellin me this. I'll watch him close, and I'll get a shot or two off—if necessary. Is he the only doctor in town?"

"There's an old-timer, Ward Bailey, but Keech took all his business away, and Ward's been mostly drunk ever since. He *was* a good man though, a good doctor. He'd work all night to save an arm or leg before he'd lop it off."

"Maybe he'll get another chance."

"If you have to smoke Keech, the town marshal will be after yuh," the barber warned. "Monk Moncrief's about the only friend Keech has got in these parts."

"Thanks again." Ram held out his hand. "My name's Rammel."

"Joe Drury." The bald, pudgy little man gripped the

hand hard. "All the luck in the world, son."

Ram smiled warmly at him. "I'll be seeing you, Joe." He started for the door and paused. "By the way, Joe, who or what were the men Keech killed?"

"They were husbands of the women Keech had used and then throwed out," Joe Drury said, without hesitation.

"In every instance?"

"Every single goddamn one of 'em."

Rammel slowly nodded his golden head. "You know, Joe, I think this town might be a lot better off without Doc Keech." He spoke in a soft lazy drawl. "If you see Doctor Ward Bailey around, tell him to start sobering up and get ready to go back to work."

"Damn right I will, Ram," said Joe Drury. "And he can do it, too. I know he can. This town ain't really had a doctor since Ward quit practice. Keech is a rep-tile. You look out for yourself, son."

"That's the ticket, Joe." Rammel grinned as he realized he had used one of Lash's pet phrases without thinking.

The Keech place, one street off the square, was a large, two-storied clapboard house painted canary yellow with maroon trim, a fancy fanlighted entrance at the center of a pillared gallery, fronted by winter-browned lawns and withered flowerbeds. The doctor must have grown rich in this poor town.

Rammel clanged the brass knocker, and a slender, white-dressed mulatto girl opened the door after an interval. "Do you have an appointment?" She was very pretty, but acted as if she were in a trance. Rammel could imagine how Keech enslaved her sexually.

"No, I really came to see Miss Ashley."

"That's impossible. The patient's sleeping and must not be disturbed."

"I'm sorry but I must insist." Rammel showed her his silver-ringed star. "I'm a Ranger."

"Well, I'll call the doctor. Please come in out of the cold."

With relief, Rammel stepped into a dimly lit entry hall, closing the heavy oak door behind him. "Wait here please." The girl indicated a long leather settee and disappeared through a yellow-draped archway. Rammel pulled off his warm-lined corduroy jacket, and hung it and his hat on the hall-tree. Knowing Keech would keep him waiting, Ram sat down and lit a cheroot.

It was ten minutes before the doctor appeared, a short thick-set form with abnormally wide shoulders and long arms, in a starched white jacket, orange silk shirt open at the bull-neck, and black pressed trousers. No guns showed, but thanks to Drury Ram could visualize one under his belt, another tucked up his sleeve on a spring contraption. His head of curling hair was too large for his body, and his gross features too big for his head. He was ugly all right, except for the brilliant magnetic eyes and perfect white teeth, offset by the vulture-beaked nose and pout-lipped mouth.

"You cannot see Miss Ashley," Keech stated in strong confident tones. "She is sleeping under sedation."

"I have a message from her family," Rammel said gently.

"She's in no condition to hear about the destruction of her home."

"This has no reference to that." Ram stood over him, tall and slim.

"It makes no difference. She's not to be seen, Ranger."

Rammel's green eyes fixed steadily on the liquid black ones. "It's important that I talk to her. I represent the state of Texas."

Keech's smile was contemptuous. "I know you're a Ranger. But in the field of medicine and my own private hospital, my authority exceeds yours, boy. Especially since we're *not* in Texas."

"I don't believe so," Rammel drawled mildly. "I intend to see the patient."

"You are leaving these premises at once." Keech's brazen face darkened even more. "I have a direct line to the marshal's office. All I have to do is press a button and Marshal Moncrief will be here to eject you."

So that's how the self-defense cases were rigged. Those poor cuckolded husbands were murdered right here in this room, without a doubt. . . . "A town marshal doesn't eject a Texas Ranger."

"This is New Mexico," reminded Keech. "A Texas Ranger doesn't mean a thing up here. You're just another trespasser."

"Call your marshal then," Rammel invited. "I'd heard you were man enough to handle your own matters, but I guess that's not the case."

"I could handle you, sonny. But a medical man shouldn't have to stoop to personal violence." Keech was beginning to smolder, his hypnotic gaze fixed on Ram's clean-cut face and holstered Colt. Rammel was slouched and easy, hands on hips, making not the slightest move toward his exposed weapon.

"You've stooped several times before, I understand," Ram said. "And then called Moncrief to label it self-defense."

"Why you snooping sonofabitch!" snarled Keech, still motionless, and behind him a girl with sagging brown head and glazed hazel eyes had appeared, wavering between the drapes, clutching the saffron velvet on either side to support herself. A deeply drugged young woman who must be Donna Ashley.

As Rammel's green eyes flicked to her, Keech made

his move, whipping his right arm forward so that a derringer jumped into his palm. Anticipating this, Rammel's right hand streaked to the .44 under his left shoulder, and it was clear, lined, and blasting loud crimson flame a second before the little pistol spat fire. The kick of the Colt jarred Ram's arm.

Ram saw Keech smashed backward, a red splotch on his snowy jacket, and felt the hot passage of lead. The girl screamed over the merging explosions, and Keech, balance recovered on spread shaking legs, tried to lift the derringer. Rammel shot him again, straight through the brutal face, and Keech's second bullet struck the ceiling, loosing a shower of plaster as the doctor crashed to the floor on the back of his neck, limbs jerking spasmodically even after death. Smoke swirled in the lamplight.

The colored girl had arrived to hold Donna upright, and the fear was gone from her handsome tan face, giving way to relief, thanksgiving and then satisfaction. Donna's eyes had cleared somewhat, and the expression on her stricken features was similar to that of the other girl's.

"Thank God, thank God," they sobbed, almost in unison, and Rammel knew that Donna Ashley had been held against her will, and the pretty mulatto had also been a captive.

"Get her back to bed, miss," Rammel said kindly. "Are you a nurse? Give her what she needs then. I'll be standing by."

He reloaded the two chambers and replaced the Colt in its shoulder holster. Finding an old Saltillo blanket, he threw it over the bloodied corpse on the floor. He couldn't feel any remorse over killing the bastard, but there was an inevitable twinge just the same. The bitter taste of gunpowder was rank in his mouth. Ram relit the cigar as an antidote.

The door-knocker clanked and startled him. Rammel pulled his hip-gun and called, "Come in." A stubby man with a hard cold face, wearing a buffalo coat, entered with a pistol in hand, but Ram's .44 was pointed straight at him. The fur and inner coat were open, revealing a marshal's badge on the vest. The man gazed into the muzzle and wagged his head.

"Put away the gun, Moncrief," said Rammel. "You haven't got a chance."

Monk acknowledged that truth and sheathed his weapon. "Christ Almighty, you killed Keech?" He gaped at the blanket-covered body. "I never thought nobody could take the doctor."

"He's dead. And I wouldn't mind dropping you beside him. From what I hear, that's where you belong. You've been covering his crimes for years."

"What crimes, for chrisake? The man was a doctor," blustered Moncrief.

"The man was a killer, and a sadistic one," Rammel said, with quiet intensity. "He murdered the husbands of women he'd drugged and raped. He amputated arms and legs that could've been saved by any kid intern. You wanta see what he did to the young Ashley girl, I'll show you right here. And you were his accomplice, Monk, guilty as hell!"

"Oh Jesus, Oh Christ!" Moncrief groaned, crumpling and shrinking inside the buffalo robe. "I never hurt nobody, but I hadda do what Keech said. He had somethin on me, he was blackmailin me, I hadda go along with him, so help me God!"

"I'm a Texas Ranger," said Rammel. "Don't tell me it means nothing up here. This gun is all I need to bank on, and *that* means something anywhere in the United States. Until I meet a faster one, and you aren't that. I'm reporting this to the Deputy U.S. Marshal over in Roswell. I may not prefer charges against you, Monk, if you don't interfere with me. Call this self-defense, which it sure as hell was. You know Keech always sneaked the first move with that sleeve-gun."

"I'll do anythin, anythin you say, Ranger," promised Moncrief. "I had to protect Keech, in order to save my own neck. But I never did nothin else wrong, I swear to God. I'm glad the rotten sonofabitch is dead. I shoulda gunned him down myself, long ago, but I didn't have the guts. I'm with you all the way, mister."

"All right, Monk. I'm inclined to believe you, for some reason. I think Keech forced you to work with him and cover for him. But don't get any ideas about crossing or backshooting me, Marshal. I'll shoot you as dead as Keech, you get outa line one inch."

"You won't turn me in then? I'll be a good peace officer, now that Keech is gone. I was always a good town marshal until Keech got that hold over me."

"I won't bring any charges against you, Monk, if you straighten out and do your job right here," Rammel told him.

Moncrief shucked off his heavy coat, sank down on the settee, and clasped his rough unshaven face in grimy hands. "Thank you and thank the Good Lord," he said piously. "Now I can start livin again, a free man, an honest man, a good man."

"You'll see that Keech fired both barrels of the derringer."

"You must be hellfire with that iron, Ranger." Moncrief looked up with awe and admiration. "Them others never had time to pull a trigger against Doc Keech." He bit off a chaw of tobacco and chewed happily. "Here's one case I can swear on the Bible was self-defense, and not be lyin my goddamn ass off."

FIVE

The storm had passed, the weather warmed, and most of
the snow had melted away by the time the Ranger trio of
Bouchard, Edley, and Travers reached El Paso. The Rio
Grande was swollen high, wide and yellow, the lesser
streams and *acequias* gushing and overrunning their
banks. They had doffed their heavy jackets in favor of
lighter ones, and gloves were no longer needed. Now
and then breezes took on a sharp cutting edge, but for
the most part it was mild and pleasant under the pale
winter sun. Bouchard and Travers agreed it was like early spring up in New England.

In town they stabled their horses in the Franklin livery barn and took rooms in the hotel, which had a
barbershop and washroom in the basement. There were
frontiersmen who went months without bathing, but the
Big Five liked to feel, look, and smell clean. They went
downstairs for the full treatment: haircuts, shaves
(beard-trimming for Bouchard), and baths. In the deep
sudsy casks they scrubbed, splashed, laughed, and
played about like kids, passing a bottle from one to another. Changing into clean town clothes they felt fresh
and immaculate, sparkling new. The bathroom atten-

44

dant told them Caldwell's three Rangers were missing, but big Rube was still on the job. El Paso was crime-ridden.

At supper in the hotel dining hall, they wrangled over plans of procedure. Rusty Bouchard had to see someone who always knew what was going on in El Paso and Juarez. To avoid being hoorawed by his friends, he did not admit that his informant was Lily Lavoy. Fox Edley finally agreed to visit the Caldwell home, contrary to his wishes, while Milt Travers would go to the Rangers' office. The proprietor said that Lashtrow and Rammel had not checked in yet, which was not surprising. The blizzard must have caught them in the Sacramento Mountains.

Over dessert and coffee, brandy and cigars, the three men grew quiet and introspective. Traveling with Travers Rangers lived high, for Trav had unlimited private funds and spent freely and gladly. Fox Edley was apprehensive about seeing Susan Hope Caldwell, the one woman he'd been ready to marry. Bouchard was wondering if and when he'd find Quadah, the Apache who had killed his gentle devoted Osage wife in the Nations. Travers, debating Priscilla Cabot's proposition, skimmed through the El Paso *Times* and understood why an aura of fear and horror hung over this community. There were two murders, two rapes and several robberies reported in this issue. Common nightly occurrences, the article concluded.

There was also a story about the many ranches in El Paso County being abandoned after losing all their cattle and horses to border raiders. Wincing at the plethora of typographical errors in the newsprint, Milt Travers handed the paper across the table. "It's even worse than we thought, boys."

"It says here a syndicate is buyin up them busted

45

spreads," Fox Edley said. "For practically nothin, I reckon."

"I'll find out tonight who's in that syndicate," Rusty Bouchard prophesied.

"I'll bet I could name most of the bastards right here and now," the Fox murmured, his amber eyes flaring in his broken-nosed face. "With Hook Cano's gang stealin the herds for 'em."

Travers nodded gravely. "We drew some assignment this time. The odds are even worse than usual. I should've resigned before this one—if I'm going to re-sign at all."

"Yeah, you're crazy to be in this jamboree, Trav," said Bouchard, "when you could be ridin the rails north to Massachusetts and a life of ease and married bliss."

"Quien sabe?" Travers flashed his charming smile. "It's all in the hands of that great jester—fate. So what the hell?"

Later, Bouchard stood on the broad front porch of the Franklin Hotel and watched Travers and Edley walk away on the elevated plank sidewalk under the streetlamps and canopied arcades. There was little activity or movement, even here in the business district. People were becoming afraid to venture out at night since this reign of terror started. The winter stars glittered frostily above the blunt humped heights of Franklin.

Travers was tall, elegant, and graceful, Edley a lean whipthong figure on bowed legs. Their backgrounds couldn't have been more different, yet they were close as brothers. Bouchard himself was a solid oak stump of a man, wide and powerful, dignified and distinguished with his neatly trimmed auburn hair and beard, velvet brown eyes and air of composure. Since his recent exploit in Wiergate, East Texas, in which he had killed three Mexican *pistoleros* of note, Rusty Bouchard was considered practically on a par with Lashtrow and Travers as a gunfighter. He knew that Edley and Rammel were just as good. There wasn't much to choose among any of Cactus Bill McKenna's favored five.

Returning to the lobby, Bouchard turned into a corridor leading to the hotel bar, and his heart rose at the sight of Lily Lavoy alone at her alcove table, proud and regal as a golden-haired queen. Rising with a radiant smile, Lily welcomed him with open arms and a kiss on the bearded lips. "Red Bush! I've been expecting you for days. You're looking great, you old hermit."

"So are you, Lil. The storm held us up a mite." Bouchard ordered a bottle of the best cognac, and sat down opposite the woman. "How are things in The Pass?"

"Couldn't be worse, Rusty," said Lily Lavoy. "Three Rangers missing over a week now. Rube Caldwell going slowly insane. Crime rampant in town and on the range."

"It must be hell on Rube." Bouchard poured brandy into two glasses.

"Worse than that. The other day Rube blew up and decided to invade Juarez singlehanded. Lucky I ran into him, or he'd be gone with his three Rangers. We rode across the river together and hit every dive and joint and cantina. No sign of Hook Cano or any of his tophands. A lot of the smaller rabble around, but no trouble. I have a sort of immunity over there, I don't know why. I let Rube think it was because he's a Ranger captain, but those animals couldn't care less about Rangers."

"The big ones musta gone up to hit the Ashley ranch in New Mexico. Lash and Rammel was sent up there first to help the Ashleys, but they was likely too late."

"I know Hook's always hounded Ash," said Lily. "He tried to make it with Amanda Ashley once, and she spit in his eye. So they burnt Ash out here in Texas, and now they've gone up to bust him again in New Mexico."

"Is there an Apache named Quadah ridin for Cano now?"

Lily inclined her blonde head. "He's one of the worst, along with Tatum, Pablito, and Fasaro. You know this Quadah, Red Bush?"

"He's the one who killed Singin Bird." Bouchard's rugged features and mild brown eyes hardened to rock, and he took a long drink. "How's Susan Caldwell standin up under the strain?"

"Not too well. They've drifted far apart. I thought it was Rube's fault, until I heard something over in Juarez. Wouldn't have believed it, but the source was good and straight. Hook Cano's been seeing Susan on the sly. He's a womanizer from way back, you know."

"Susan wouldn't take up with the likes of him," Bouchard protested.

Lily's smile was ironic. "You wouldn't believe how many so-called *good* women have fallen for that sonofabitch Cano."

"Christ at the crossroads," muttered Bouchard. "Fox Edley's gone to visit the Caldwells tonight."

"I remember when he and Rube were courting Susan, and the Fox lost out." A wisp of a smile touched her full scarlet mouth. "Or maybe the Fox won, in the final analysis. Rube's beginning to fall apart."

"What about this syndicate that's buyin up all the ranches hereabouts?"

"I have my notions," Lily said. "But I couldn't prove anything."

"What's Sheriff Kriewold doin about all these killins?"

"Nothing but making statements on how hard he and his staff are working on the cases. Krie controls the city as well as county law, but they don't do a thing but blame Rube Caldwell and the Rangers."

"Are all the victims Anglos?"

Lily nodded her gleaming head. "A hundred percent, Red Bush. We need a company or two of cavalry, and they send us five Rangers. I know you're the best, but what can five men do against Hook Cano's horde?"

"I don't know, Lil." Bouchard shrugged his great shoulders and lit another cheroot, after holding the match to Lily's brown cigarillo. "Gimme your idea of the syndicate."

She sighed. "What good'll it do, Rusty? You can't touch any of them."

"Maybe we'll find a way to get at 'em. Let's hear some names, sweet."

"You already know 'em," Lily Lavoy said. "Sheriff Kriewold, Mayor Amos Essling, Judge Milo Bascomb, Leo Fribance, and Yaeger, the stockyard man."

"Yeah, that's about what we figgered," Bouchard admitted. "The big augurs of El Paso." He bowed his head, streaked with fire in the lamplight, and brooded morosely over his glass.

"What's the matter, dear Red Bush?"

"This situation is so goddamn hopeless. I wonder that Rube hasn't cracked long ago."

"So do I, darling," Lily said. "But the odds never bothered you much. There's something more."

"We could be losin Milt Travers."

"Well, Trav should be writing books instead of chasing greasers. I read his novel, *Men and Guns,* and it was damn good. I read a lot, Rusty, and I know good writing. Trav's really got it. He's wasting his life with the Rangers."

"I know that, Lil," Bouchard said. "But I hate to see him go."

"Of course you do. Travers is a fine boy. But you've all got something bigger to worry about here. A little matter of survival."

49

"Yeah, we know that, too. But it's nothin real new to us. An old story, so we don't fret too much about it." He sipped glumly at his brandy, with sadness in his deep brown eyes.

"This is supposed to be a gay happy reunion, Red Bush. You're letting me down, old pard." Her laughing voice was light and merry.

"Never," he said absently, the sorrow still with him.

Lily Lavoy studied him, her green eyes suddenly soft and tender. She inspected the jeweled rings on her shapely hands, and spoke almost shyly, "You're lonesome and sad, Rusty. You need cheering up. Take me up to your room."

"I can't afford you, lady." Bouchard grinned through his red beard.

"I never charged you, did I?" Lily demanded with some indignation. "I'm not working this week anyway. If you ever tried to pay me, I'd blow your stupid red head off!"

"It wouldn't do any good, Lil."

"We can just sit around and talk over a bottle. It'll be any way you want it, man. I'm lonely too, goddamn it! And I've always liked you, Red Bush. We always liked one another—I thought."

"Sure we have, baby." Bouchard's eyes brightened and warmed. "We always will. Put a coupla these glasses in your handbag, and I'll take the bottle. If it ain't enough, I got another in my saddlebags."

As they walked to the stained-glass door opening on the side street, other male customers watched with envy and interest. Lily moved like a lady of royal lineage, grace and pride in every stride, her golden head high and shimmering under the crystal chandeliers, and Bouchard was a solid imposing shape at her side. No remarks were passed until the door closed behind them. The night air was keen and fresh on their faces.

"What if they try to stop us at the desk?" Bouchard wondered. "I don't wanta have to shoot a desk clerk."

"They won't," Lily said. "I go where I please in this town."

The room was bare and plain, but clean and tidy enough. Safely ensconced within the locked door, they removed outer garments and settled down in the low-turned lampglow. There were a scarred dresser and table, a worn armchair and a rather fragile rocker, which Lily selected. The bed occupied most of the chamber, but they disregarded it for the moment. The privacy was welcome, and Lily's perfumed presence made the place seem cozy, secure, and homey.

They chatted and drank pleasantly for an hour, and then Lily Lavoy started to cast yearning glances at the bed. "I won't ravish you, darling," she promised playfully. "I'll just hold you in my arms and comfort you." They undressed and got into bed, and for an interval it was as she had said. They rested drowsily in a loose embrace, until desire rose and inflamed them. Lily had a superb body, and Bouchard hadn't possessed a woman in some time. It was inevitable that a sweet flame consumed them, welding them tight and hot together, the man plunged deeply into the lush moist depths of the woman, her arms and legs crushing him ever closer, weaving an exotic pattern of pleasure and delight, obliterating all else in the ultimate union of the flesh.

Lily Lavoy was highly skilled, a paragon in the art of bringing rare and total satisfaction, holding nothing back and sharing fully in the rapture. They climaxed together, then drifted into slumber.

SIX

At the log cabin in the Sacramentos, the Anvil party and Lashtrow stayed two days to rest, recuperate and round up the stock. The first morning after the storm dawned clear and cold, the sun rising pale and heatless, but gaining color and warmth as it climbed the eastern sky over the Guadalupes. By noon the snow began to melt, the cattle foraging through it for grass. The creek overflowed its banks. Ice-sheathed willows along the stream glistened and shed crystal drops. All around the valley the peaks were white-frosted, brilliant against the blue horizon.

Arizona wanted to get up and help with the work, but once on his feet he was dizzy and faint, his eyes blurred with concussion, and Lash put him back to bed with a stern admonition to stay there. He wasn't ready to travel, and some of the weaker cows and horses had to be nursed back to health before resuming the drive.

The Ashleys were a fine couple, generous and considerate, honest and sincere. The love and loyalty of their four riders were a testimonial to that. Ash was a long lank man with steady solemn eyes and hollow leathery cheeks. Amanda was a gracious, gallant woman, her faded blue eyes frank and clear, her face still

52

young and comely under gray-flecked brown hair. They worried about their daughter Donna, but Lashtrow assured them that Rammel would care for her like a big brother with a beloved sister. And hoped that he was right.

On their second day in the basin the weather was much warmer. With the snow going fast, the stock grazed and filled up at will on the grassland and water. Cobb and Mullen butchered the few cows that had died, and Amanda fried some delicious steak meals. Arizona was sitting up and eating with appetite, the danger past and strength returning to his sinewy frame. Lash required him to take it easy, and Arizona affectionately called him "Doc," with a gay reckless grin, that was in direct contrast to Val Verde's acid sour mien. Youngsters with such nicknames were generally gunfighters, who rode for fighting wages and left gaudy reputations somewhere behind, but they were good boys, or they wouldn't be working for the Ashleys.

Cobb and Mullen were older and more settled hands, affable and dependable enough, but without the exuberance of Arizona and Val Verde. There'd been three other cowboys on Anvil, but they had elected to draw their pay and pull out, after the spread was burned down by the *bandidos*. These four had a sense of loyalty that money could not buy.

The third morning they started the trail drive again, with Amanda on the Schuttler wagon seat and Arizona bedded down in back under the hood, much to his vociferous disgust and dismay. Lashtrow rode at the front, alert against ambushes. Behind the creaking vehicle, Ashley lured out his old lead steer and built his point, with Cobb and Mullen swinging on the flanks and Val Verde pushing the drag. The trained *remuda* drifted behind.

At a lunch break, Lashtrow spoke to Ashley. "If you decide not to sell you could prob'ly buy a layout cheap in El Paso County. A lot of ranchers have lost their herds, and are moving out."

"Not even if I had the money, Lash," said Ashley. "Cano'd hit us again, as soon as we got settled in. Besides, I heard there's one outfit buyin up all them spreads."

"Where'd you hear that, Ash?"

"From Doc Keech back in Pinon. He's investin money down in El Paso, hooked up with what they call the syndicate. Says he'll be rich enough to retire in a year or two."

"Retire from what?" Val Verde scoffed. "He ain't no doctor, Ash. He's a goddamn stud hoss. A pal of mine had a bullet-grazed arm, nothin but a burn really. Keech claimed gangrene set in and he hadda chop off that arm. Keech is an asshole."

"I never believed all them stories about him, Val," said Ashley.

"I heard so many I hadda believe 'em," Val Verde declared, with Mullen and Cobb nodding in agreement. "Keech is a no-good varmint," Mullen said.

"Well, I don't know," Ashley mumbled. "Our first concern now is gettin these cattle and horses to El Paso."

"Two more days on the trail will do it," Lashtrow drawled. "But I got a feeling those Mexes'll hit us before we get in there. They won't get the herd though." The bronzed skin was drawn taut over his cheek and jawbones.

Arizona shouted a complaint from the wagon tailgate. "When do I get outa here and onto a bronc, for chrisake? I'm about as much use here as a burr in a hoss's tail. Old Doc Lashtrow sure likes to pamper and pet his patients."

"Quit cryin, crowbait!" Val Verde yelled back heartlessly. "We got enough trouble without you fallin off any more hosses."

"You'll have trouble, you little sheepdog," Arizona promised. "When I get back on my feet."

The drive went on through the mountain passes. The higher slopes and crests still shone dazzling white, but the open cuts were bare and almost snowless by this time. The drovers made fair time, despite the highland terrain, but Lashtrow had a sense of impending disaster.

About a day out of El Paso, it started snowing again, but lightly and softly at this lower altitude, with none of the unleashed fury of the mountain blizzard. Lash fell back of the lumbering Schuttler to ride for a moment with Ashley at the point of the herd. A bend in the canyon brought the wagon back into view, halted in the trace with a half-dozen Mexican horsemen before the six-mule team, blocking the way.

"Cano's bunch," Ashley said, checking the lead steers and drawing his Henry rifle from its scabbard.

Lashtrow unbuttoned his jacket to clear the holstered Colts, and pulled his Winchester from the boot. Cobb and Mullen galloped up from their swing positions to the point, which was halted and bawling. Val Verde was too far back with the *remuda* and drag to see what was going on. The Mexicans sat their ornamented saddles calm and unthreatening, but with carbines across the pommels. A rugged good-looking white man seemed to be the leader.

"There's more than six of 'em," Lashtrow said. "Flanking us in the brush and fir trees."

Ashley was identifying them for Lash: "Tatum, the big one, white but of mixed blood. Fasaro, the slick weasel in fancy clothes. Pablito, the hoptoad, a mad-dog killer. The Injun's Quadah. Can't name the other two. Oh yeah, one's called Chacon."

"They don't really wanta fight here," Lashtrow said, scanning the enemy array with slitted green eyes. "Unless we show fear." He led the way forward on his rangy sorrel. At the rear of the Schuttler he said: "Arizona, they're here. Watch the back area."

"I got it, Doc," said Arizona through the canvas.

The four spread out and moved forward to the front of the wagon. Amanda Ashley, reins wrapped around the whipstock, held a shotgun across her knees and faced the men who had burned her home, without a hint of fear or panic. The Mexicans were surprised, and not pleasurably, to see the tall bleak-faced stranger on the golden sorrel. They read what he was in the set of his tawny head and wide shoulders, the strong-boned features, the easy assurance of his whole manner, the weapons that were part of him.

"You have a new hand, Señor Ashley," said Tatum, his tone courteous and pleasant, his smile serene. "Happy to see you survived the blizzard—and saved your cattle. We had thought to be of assistance perhaps."

"Don't be ridiculous, Tatum," grated Ashley. "You want war, let it start here. What the hell *do* you want?"

"Why nothing, nothing at all, my friend." Tatum was suave and smooth as oil. "Simply an exchange of greetings on the road to El Paso."

"Get out then," Ashley said, cold and quiet. "Out of our way and on your own, amigo."

"You are hostile, Señor Ashley." Tatum's smile broadened, a flash of white across his rather handsome face. "We do not want your herd. We could have taken it earlier and easier, had that been our intention. But that long hard drive through the mountains did not appeal to us. You know we are a lazy people."

"We waste time here," Fasaro said, the tiny silver bells on his steeple sombrero tinkling at the impatient jerk of his sleek head. "Let's ride, *compañeros.*"

"Ees no big hurry," Pablito protested, urging his pinto ahead and peering insolently up at Lashtrow. "Thees hombre I have interest in. Thees large gringo I have seen somewhere before." A leer crinkled his evil froglike countenance. His right elbow angled wide, and his hand hung spread-fingered in a theatrical pose. The thick accent was a put-on, too.

"Come on, come on, Pablito," said Fasaro, in disgust.

Lashtrow stared intently at the squat ugly Mexican. "You want me to draw on you?"

"Why not, *caballero?*" jeered Pablito.

"Just the two of us?"

"Ees enough. One against one."

Lashtrow shook his finely shaped head. "It'd turn into a general dog-fight. We don't want that, with a lady present."

"Ah, you are afraid to draw, big man." Pablito grinned gloatingly.

"There's no point in it, no sense at all," Lash drawled. "We have no reason to fight—yet."

"I geeve reason, gringo sonofabitch!" Pablito snarled, an insane light in his dilated protruding eyeballs.

They reached simultaneously, and Lashtrow threw the sorrel against the smaller pony. Pablito's pistol cleared leather, as he rocked off balance from the jarring collision, but Lash was quicker, his gun barrel slashing down on the Mex's wrist. Pablito screamed in pain, the weapon flying from his grasp, the horses still surging against each other. Lash's left hand caught Pablito by the throat, lifted him from the saddle, and hurled him to earth. Pablito bounced on the ground, air and consciousness beaten from his body, which slumped into stillness.

"No shooting, no shooting!" cried Tatum, taking command once more with an imperious gesture. "Hold your fire. Pablito is crazy, a complete idiot. Chacon, get him back onto his horse."

The Anvil riders had their long guns leveled at the Mexicans, who were booting their carbines under the whip of Tatum's tongue. Amanda was holding the double-barreled Greener on Tatum himself, her brown hands white-knuckled.

Colt in hand, Lashtrow's green gaze was on Tatum. "Call the rest of your crew outa the woods."

Behind the wagon to the right, a mounted rifleman emerged from stunted pines and spruces and took careful aim at Lashtrow's back. Arizona's Winchester crashed and flamed over the tailboard, blowing the Mexican off the pony's back in a gush of blood from his torn-out throat.

Another greaser came out of the evergreens on the left, switching his carbine barrel from Lashtrow toward Arizona, but Val Verde raced up from behind and hammered two swift shots into this second sniper, blasting him out of the saddle into a crimsoned bundle on a patch of snow. Receding hoofbeats sounded from the woods, as other unseen ambushers fled the scene, and the tableau up front remained static.

"Saved your friggin life," Val Verde grumbled, as he made certain the two snipers were dead.

"Balls!" said Arizona, grinning over the tailgate. "I had 'em both, if you hadn't horned in."

Up ahead of the mule team, Chacon had the semiconscious Pablito roped on the pinto, and was back on his own bronc.

"I regret very much—" Tatum started.

Ashley interrupted, "We oughta kill all you bastards! If my wife wasn't watchin, we'd shoot you all down. Clear out before we do."

"Don't let me stop you, dear," Amanda said, from the wagon seat.

"Andale!" cried Tatum. "Come on, fools, before you get us all killed."

Val Verde had jogged up alongside the others. "You got two dead bushwhackers back there. Don't you want 'em?"

"Let 'em rot," Fasaro said. "Let the buzzards have 'em."

"We're moving on," Tatum said. "But we'll see you later—in El Paso."

Lashtrow nodded grimly. "You can count on that."

The Mexicans wheeled and cantered away in a south-westerly course toward El Paso. The mounts of the dead snipers broke out of the brush and trotted after them. In retreat they looked neither defeated nor troubled.

Lashtrow sighed in relief. "We got outa that one a lot better than it figured. Thanks to Arizona and Val Verde. Nice shooting, boys."

"Hell, they was settin ducks," Val Verde said.

The husky Cobb looked at Lashtrow in awe. "Pablito never got handled that way before, Lash. S'posed to be all-hell with a sixgun. He'll never live that down."

"He ain't got long to live anyway," Mullen gritted.

"All right, boys, let's get 'em goin again," Ashley said.

"I'll stay up front with you, Amanda," called Lash. "But I don't think they'll be coming back."

The drive rolled on again, winding downward through foothills now. The light snowfall had ended, without anyone noticing. They were in the homestretch and spirits were rising, but El Paso was no sanctuary.

"Very fortunate you were with us, Lash," said Amanda, over the grind of axles and rumble of wheels, mingled with chopping hooves.

"I didn't do much."

"You didn't have to. They were scared when they saw

you. I could tell from their eyes."

Lashtrow laughed. "That shotgun of yours prob'ly scared 'em as much as anything, Amanda."

In the distance they could see the blurred amber glow of El Paso, on its mesa at the foot of Mt. Franklin, and the deep-notched pass of the Rio Grande. The sun was gone, the winter air blue and gray with dusk.

"I always think of the old Spanish *conquistadores* in their armor, the first white men to ride through El Paso del Norte," said Amanda. "Thousands of miles from home, hunting for fabled cities of gold."

Lashtrow nodded in sympathy, having had such visions himself. "They say one of the first was probably the explorer, Onate, a couple of hundred years ago. The old Chihuahua Trail followed his route up to Santa Fe. Then came Comanche horse thieves and Apache raiders, the Butterfield stagecoach line and the Goodnight-Loving cattle trail. Now the railroad will run through the pass."

"Yes, I can see them all, coming and searching and dying through the years," Amanda said dreamily. "Seeking some kind of treasure, and finding death. It goes on over and over, generation after generation, and what does it mean, Lash? What does it all amount to?"

He raised broad shoulders and shook his sandy head. "All we know for sure is there is but one ending, the same for everybody. You live the best you can, until that time comes for you. Then the last great adventure starts —or there is nothing more, nothing at all."

"Oh, it's all so sad and hopeless."

"It is sad," Lash agreed. "But not quite hopeless. As long as you're alive."

The next day, eyes and head cleared, Arizona was back in the saddle, happy as a child at Christmas, brightening up the whole crew with his kidding and laughing. El Paso was a real city, compared to Pinon, and Arizona and Val Verde were excited by the prospects. Even Cobb and Mullen were stirred by the possibilities of celebrating the end of the drive. "Goin to find me a wife in The Pass," said Mullen, with a homely grin.

"I hope Huffnail and Millhauser are there to close the deal, as they promised," said Ashley.

"It's late in the day. They may not be there." Lashtrow had a hunch the buyers would not be on hand. The way things were in El Paso at present, the herd might be stolen that very night.

As the Schuttler wagon and strung-out cattle neared town, Ashley rode on ahead to make arrangements at the Yeager Stockyards, on the low-lying outskirts in a poorer section of town. It was too close to the Mexican quarter and the Rio Grande, Lash realized, with no one but the regular attendants to guard the stock. The Anvil cowboys couldn't be denied their night on the city; the Ashleys and Lashtrow himself were dead-tired. If the rustlers struck, they'd come in irresistible force. No way to stop them. Lashtrow had a sinking sensation in the pit of his stomach, as he pressed the point on toward the pens, dry dust boiling around them.

Ashley was waiting by the gates. "They ain't here, Lash," he said. "And Yeager can't—or won't—take responsibility for the herd. Huffnail and Millhauser will be here with the money in the mornin'."

He and Lashtrow joined the others in punching the cattle into the stockyards. Val Verde drove his *remuda* to a horse corral. The wide expanse of railed pens had been vacant, until the arrival of this trail herd. Lash felt bitterly that they were making delivery to the bandits of Hook Cano, just as the outlaw chief had planned. The bleat of animals was a mournful sound.

He hoped that Caldwell was all right, that Travers, Bouchard, and Edley had already joined Rube here in El Paso.

SEVEN

The Caldwell home was a trim brick structure on one of the higher northern levels of El Paso, a nice residential district, the houses well-spaced behind trees, hedges and lawns. Mellow lamplight glowed from windows, and the roofed wooden gallery was strewn with children's toys and playthings. Unlike Susan to leave any place cluttered. Fox Edley had to wait quite a while for the front door to open. Susan stood there limned in soft yellow light, her face without any expression of surprise or pleasure or welcome. A dead face and dead eyes, Edley thought, shocked by the drastic change in her.

"Why, Foxcroft, come in." Her voice was flat and lifeless, too. "Sorry to keep you waiting. I just finished putting the children to bed."

"Hullo, Susan." He removed his hat and stepped inside. He had imagined many versions of this meeting, but none like this. "Where's Rube?"

"In his office—or study. He spends all his time there —when he's home. Which is not too often." Her laugh was brittle, as she led him into the parlor, a comfortably furnished room, but littered like the porch. She pointed to a worn leather easy chair. "Please sit down. I guess you'd prefer a drink to coffee?"

"Yeah, I haven't changed that much, Susie."

"But you think *I* have? I can read it in your cat-eyes."

"No, not really," Edley murmured. "You're still a fine-lookin woman." She was handsome as ever, but the sparkle was gone. Her gray eyes and proud features had taken on a hardness that Edley had noticed in other wives who were not in love with their husbands. Almost the look of whores, he mused, and perhaps natural and inevitable. They'd traded their bodies for matrimony, a home and a living. It wasn't so different from prostitution. Some no doubt were efficient wives and mothers.

"Well, *you* don't look any older, Foxcroft. It's truly amazing." She poured liquor from a crystal decanter into two glasses. She hadn't liked to drink in the old days, hadn't needed the stimulation.

"I never looked that young anyhow," Edley said, with his crooked grin. "Hit too many times in the face with everythin from fists and bottles to clubs and knives."

"But you always had those golden eyes and that smile, Fox." For an instant she showed a flare of animation, the old gaiety, and then it vanished. She subsided into a dull remoteness, became an apathetic stranger.

"How is Rube standin this war with Mexico?" Edley sipped his drink and found it excellent.

"Not very well." Susan sighed and bowed her lustrous dark head. "His three men are still missing. Dead and buried in Mexican soil by now, but Rube won't admit it. He's all alone. No help from the city police or county sheriff's staff. No cooperation from the *Rurales* across the river. Too much for one man alone. It's driving him insane, Fox, breaking him to pieces."

"I know, Susan. It's too much for any one man. Nobody could handle it. Anyone but Rube would have quit long before now."

"He's as stubborn as ever. Nothing'll ever change

Rube Caldwell." She took a long swallow, almost draining the glass. It seemed to go down like water, and Edley knew this was another thing that had coarsened her. "I'll go and call him." She laughed harshly. "He'll most likely tell me to shut up, beat it, leave him alone."

"Yeah, I don't reckon he's too anxious to see me," Edley drawled, with a wry twist to his lips.

"Oh, I'm sure he'll be glad to see you, Fox. I'm the one he doesn't care to see."

"It's the job, Sue. He always took it too big, too serious."

"I know it, Foxcroft. That's absolutely true. How are the other boys? Big Lash, good old Red Bush, and the beautiful Travers."

"Still alive and well, by the grace of God," said Fox Edley. "Trav and Red Bush are here with me. Lash and a boy named Rammel are comin down from New Mexico. Trav writes books now, you know."

"Yes, I read his book of poems. It was lovely. Trav has everything. All that money and talent and looks. Everything."

"And regular as an old boot," Edley added. "They're all great men. I mean *great,* Susan. Thank God I fell in with 'em. A beat-up bronc peeler, outlaw, and gunman with my record."

The woman's gray eyes and sharp features softened for a moment. "You're as great as any of them, Foxcroft." She lifted her glass. "To all of you Rangers." Her face hardened once more, and her gaze went far away.

Then abruptly, an awkward silence prevailed and they were strangers again, worlds and light-years apart. Susan refilled their glasses, and drank half of hers at a gulp, obviously reluctant to go call her husband. Edley could think of nothing to say. She had gone too far away to reach with words. He felt a compulsion to take her in his arms, but quickly put it down. He'd never made·a play for another man's wife, and he never would. That was a code Fox and his friends lived by.

At last Susan spoke, with an effort. "Well, I'll tell Rube you are here."

"That'll prob'ly keep him in his office," Edley said dryly.

"No, he still likes you, Fox. He talks a lot about you —and the other boys. He admires and respects you all." She finished her drink and walked out of the room, a shapely woman with deep breasts and hips, moving with lissome grace. With more sexuality than Fox remembered.

She was gone a long time, and Edley poured himself a fresh drink, nervously pacing the carpeted floor. In the small bookcase, he saw *Wuthering Heights, Jane Eyre, Pamela, Lorna Doone,* and then a copy of Travers's thin volume of verse, *Somewhere Back of the Sun.* Taking it out he looked at the dedication: *To All Ladies of Shalott.* Trav had told him the sad story of Elaine, the Lily Maid, and Lancelot, a knight of the Round Table in King Arthur's Camelot. Trav said the Rangers were a lot like those ancient knights, without the shields, swords, and armor. It made Fox prouder than ever of being a Ranger. In their cups they sometimes called each other Sir Trav and Sir Fox.

When Susan returned she was visibly agitated and distraught. "He's locked in there. He won't answer me, won't say a word. I thought I could smell gunpowder. Oh God in heaven!"

"Show me the way, Sue," said Edley. "Don't fret. Maybe he's takin a nap in there. Sleepin so sound he didn't hear you."

She led him along dim corridors to a room at the rear of the house. Edley rapped loudly and called, "Rube!

65

Wake up, Rube! You got company." There was no response, not a sound. A cold tremor fluttered in Fox's chest.

"Oh dear God!" moaned Susan Caldwell. "I'm afraid, Fox. I've been afraid of something like this." She was terrified, on the verge of fainting.

"Was he alone all evenin?" Fear spread like a chill through Edley.

"Yes. Nobody else has been here."

"Could anyone get in through the windows? Or a back door?" Edley's scalp crawled.

"No, they're locked and shuttered tight."

"Has Rube been sick or anythin?"

"Not physically. Just sick over his job and all the murders."

Fox Edley knocked and shouted again, even louder. There was no reply, no movement within the room. The door was too thick and solid to break down. Fox drew his .44. "Where's the lock?"

"It's just a bolt. There—above the doorknob."

"I'll have to shoot it off, Susan."

She nodded dazedly, too choked with emotion and terror to speak.

Fox Edley squinted at the narrow slit of light between door and jamb, and spotted the shadow of the bolt. "Hate to wake the kids." He fired through the bolt, and the door swung inward. "Jesus Christ!" Fox said softly. "I never woulda believed it." The odor of gunsmoke stained the air.

Rube Caldwell was hunched over the flat-topped desk, his shattered head lying on some carmined papers, a pistol beside his outflung right hand. His bulk was tilted to the left, his left arm hanging straight down.

"Don't look! Don't look, for chrisake!" Edley said.

Susan gasped as if mortally stricken, groaned, and slid

slack-limbed to the floor and unconsciousness before Fox could catch her. He went to the door and windows in turn, checking them out. Securely locked and steel-shuttered, no one could have gotten through them. There were no other apertures in walls, ceiling, or floor. There could be but one verdict: *Suicide.* Rube Caldwell had been shot through the right side of the skull. There was a powder-scorched entry hole, and a larger ragged exit wound, with fragments of bone and brains spattered bloodily across the desk.

"Never thought you'd do this, Rube," murmured Fox Edley. "It musta got awful bad to make you do this, old pard. I'm sorry, Rube, sorry as hell."

He lifted Susan tenderly into his arms and carried her back to the parlor, her eyes closed, her face ghastly white. Very gently he laid her down on the doeskin-covered couch. Still stunned, Fox drank straight from a cognac bottle and thought about what to do first.

Fox didn't want to go back to that office, but the telephone was there. He hated to call Sheriff Kriewold or the city police chief, Royer, because neither had been friendly or helpful to Rube. He had no faith in or use for Mayor Essling and Judge Bascomb. The news would please those bastards, and that was the last thing Fox Edley wished to do. He waited for the children to wake and start crying upstairs, but the silence remained unbroken.

There'd been no suicide note, he recalled. That wasn't like the pragmatic Captain either.

It still seemed to Fox Edley that someone somehow had killed Rube Caldwell. It was impossible, as he had observed with his own eyes, yet the idea persisted. Well, Rube was out of it, at any rate. Nothing or nobody could hurt him any more. He was gone beyond any further anguish or grief, safe and unknowing in death. It wasn't really suicide. Rangering had killed Rube Caldwell, just as it had slain so many other good men.

Fox Edley swigged from the bottle again, and went unwillingly back to the office telephone. He phoned the Rangers' office downtown, but nobody answered. He tried the Franklin Hotel, but the clerk said Bouchard and Travers were not there. Finally he called the hospital and requested an ambulance be sent to transport a dead body to the undertaker's. The woman wasn't cooperative or interested, until Fox told her he was a Texas Ranger and "wanted some goddamn action goddamn soon!"

Fox kept his gaze averted from the dead man, but even so he was gagging and retching miserably as he left the room.

Susan Caldwell had emerged from her fainting spell and was sitting up on the couch, glass in hand, despair and horror in every line of her face and form. "What am I going to do, Fox? What'll become of us now?"

"Be thankful the kids didn't wake up," Edley said, rather coldly. "You'll be taken care of." Her husband's dead, Fox thought bitterly, and all she's worrying about is herself. Didn't Rube mean a thing to her, after all those years of marriage? He avoided looking at her, as he had at Rube's body. What kind of a frigged-up world was this, for chrisake? Didn't the death of a good man mean anything—even to his wife?

"An ambulance is comin," Fox Edley said. "I'll go with Rube. You gotta stay with the kids. I'll tend to all the details, if it's okay with you."

Susan Caldwell nodded numbly, swallowed brandy, and stared emptily at the Fox, as if she'd never seen him before and didn't care to see him again. Something about her made him feel dead inside himself. *Maybe she killed Rube.*

EIGHT

Milt Travers found the second-floor Ranger office shut, locked, and dark. He banged on the door a few times, even though he knew the place was empty. Without understanding why, he was in a mean, ugly mood. Perhaps his indecision about the future caused it. Whether to stay in the Rangers, or go home and marry Priscilla Cabot and write books. Common sense dictated the latter, yet he didn't want to leave the Rangers. There were no friends anywhere like Lash, the Fox, Ram, and Red Bush. He just couldn't walk out on them—not yet anyway.

Strolling around El Paso, he was aware of the emptiness of the streets, the quietness of the saloons, gambling emporiums, restaurants, dance halls, and cantinas. A tangible aura of fear hung over the town. There were no patrols of lawmen riding about, no city cops walking beats. Here and there at scattered street corners, he saw lone uniformed policemen standing beneath lamp posts. It was a civic disgrace, considering the epidemic of crimes that had broken out here. His anger increasing at every step, Travers walked toward city hall. The county jail was just across the way.

It was a massive and homely adobe-brick building of

two stories, with many of the office windows still alight. Two sentries in sloppy blue uniforms, lolling at the main entrance, shuffled forth to intercept Travers.

"I'm a Ranger," Trav said impatiently, flashing his badge. "Is Essling still in his office?"

"They're all up there," one copper said, spitting tobacco juice. "Go ahead in, Ranger."

"They send you to take Cap'n Caldwell's place?" asked the other.

Travers strode by, not bothering to respond. The interior was dirty and slovenly. He climbed a broad creaking wooden stairway to the second floor, and located the door marked MAYOR'S OFFICE in large gilt letters.

Nobody answered his knock, so Travers thrust the door open and walked in, and was confronted by a tall bony man wearing an oversized sheriff's shield, his mouth lipless between a big beak of a nose and long lantern jaw, a sour grimace on his skeletal face. "What the hell you want here, boy?"

"I'm a Ranger," Travers said. "And a little too old to be termed a boy. My name is Milton Travers."

"Oh, yeah, I've heard a you," Sheriff Kriewold said. "What d'yuh want?"

"Why, I wanted to meet you and the mayor and the judge, all the civic leaders," Travers said with sugary sarcasm.

"C'mon, I'll interduce you. This is Ranger Travers, men."

Amos Essling sat in a huge black horsehide chair behind an enormous polished desk, fat and bald with a bland red face and politician's beaming smile. His eyes were nearly hidden by heavy dark lids and plump mottled cheeks. He raised a stubby hand in casual greeting, and pulled at his purple-veined nose.

Milo Bascomb, surprisingly young for a judge, rose to

shake hands. He was two inches taller than Trav's six feet, with direct challenging eyes and an arrogant manner. His suit was flawlessly tailored. "Welcome to El Paso, Mr. Travers."

Leo Fribance, pomaded hair as oily as his eyes, simply nodded and smiled with pulpy lips. He was a short stocky man, trying to appear dapper and debonair like Bascomb, but failing. Fribance was the Copper King of the county.

Yeager, rough and ready owner of the stockyards, offered a gnarled grimy hand and forced a smile. He was dressed in shabby range garb with a double-holstered gunbelt, his pockmarked cheeks stubbled with a dirty gray beard. Heavy-set and powerful, he smelled of the cattle pens.

All in all, the men who ran El Paso, county and town, were a pretty cast of characters, Travers decided. Save for the personable Bascomb, they could be shot for their looks alone.

"Now what can we do for you, Mr. Travers?" inquired Mayor Essling.

"Nothing for me," Trav said. "But it seems you could do a lot more for this town, if you cared to."

"What the hell you mean?" rasped Sheriff Kriewold, starting up from his chair. Bascomb waved him back with an indolent manicured hand.

Travers ignored him and went on. "I've been walking around outside. I saw no patrols, mounted or afoot, anywhere. I saw only a very few policemen, scattered far apart, leaning on street-corner lamp poles. And they say you have a murder or two every night in El Paso."

"You tryin to tell me how to run my office?" grated Kriewold.

"Someone ought to," Travers said gravely.

"I have to cover the whole county." Kriewold reared

up again, but Bascomb once more gestured him back into his chair. "Your complaint should go to the chief of police, sonny."

"Where can I find him?"

Milo Bascomb laughed aloud. "In Fat Emma's fancy house, I imagine. Royer spends most of his time there."

"Why don't you fire him and put in a real chief?" demanded Travers. No one replied. "How many deputies do you have, Sheriff?"

"Well—uh—about a dozen, I'd say."

"I heard you had twenty or thirty."

"By jeezus that's enough!" Kriewold bellowed, bouncing upright and staying this time, tall as a tree and raging mad. "Git your ass outa here, kid, before I blow it off yuh!"

"Start blowing," Travers invited coolly.

Bascomb rose between them, palms spread to both antagonists. "Gentlemen, I believe this has gone rather too far. I suggest we adjourn this unscheduled meeting, and get together later at a more propitious time. We hope to collaborate with you, Ranger Travers, but you came on pretty strong tonight, and nothing can be gained by continuing in this fashion."

His soothing and civilized speech had a cooling effect on Travers, who suddenly felt a bit ashamed of his own behavior. It had been entirely out of character for him, and his cheeks and ears were suddenly rimmed with fire.

"You're quite right, Judge Bascomb," he said politely. "I had no right to break in here with those accusations, and I apologize to all of you. I'll say good night now, and we'll meet again under more pleasant circumstances. Please forgive the intrusion and my ill manners."

Bascomb reached out to shake his hand, and Travers turned away to walk out the door, slender and straight as a lance, fair head shimmering.

Christ, I must have been crazy to pull something like that, Travers reflected as he descended the worn splintered stairs. What the hell's the matter with me anyway? The Rangers don't need any more enemies on this front, and I sure didn't gain any friends for us tonight. Except possibly Judge Bascomb, and underneath he might have resented it more than the rest of them. Bascomb was the formidable one.

Well, I'm too fired up to go to bed, and I don't want to get drunk. Better walk around some more, and maybe I'll run across a Mexican trying to rape or kill or rob some Anglo. Probably feel a lot better if I could burn down one or two of those murderous greasers. Might even restore my balance and sanity. Certainly acted like a madman tonight, and my ears are still seared from recalling it. When I lose control like that, I'm in a bad way.

Travers sauntered into a tough slum section down by the river, where there were no police and streetlamps were few and far between. Infrequent pedestrians and horsemen moved quickly and furtively. Rosy lamp-light with muted music and voices issued from some of the nightspots. In the distance he glimpsed a horse-drawn ambulance pass a lighted intersection and wondered who the victim was.

Drifting into a dreary dive called the Sierra Saloon, Travers ordered a beer at the bar and listened to the subdued talking under smoke-wreathed hanging lamps. Someone reported a trail herd coming in from New Mexico tomorrow, and Trav thought it might be the Ashleys of Anvil with Lashtrow and Rammel. Or it could be the rustlers from Hook Cano's band.

At one table a dark vivid girl was surrounded by men, laughing and joking, apparently in control of her admirers. A little cleaning up would make her beautiful, Travers realized. She had the face and figure and charm the allure. Her smile was dazzling, her laugh contagious, and she flirted outrageously with all of them. Now and then her shining dark gaze flitted to the clean, tanned features of Travers, lingered impishly, and went back to the rough-faced men encircling her. She wore a white flower in her glossy black hair.

When she rose to leave, a half-dozen cowboys tried to escort her, but the girl banished them with an imperious wave of her hand and a haughty toss of her dark head. Travers was surprised that nobody attempted to follow her. She was the likely target for a rapist, and Trav himself slipped unobtrusively from the barroom to see her safely home. There was a wildness in his blood tonight, a need for action and violence. It was a side of himself that Trav didn't particularly like, yet it had always lurked beneath the aristocratic surface.

No sidewalks existed in this area, and Travers's boots made little sound in the gravel. The girl didn't know she was being followed, and didn't seem at all afraid or apprehensive, despite recent events. She was either foolish or fearless—perhaps they were synonymous. After a block she slipped into the black mouth of an alleyway, as if taking a shortcut. Travers leaped into his smooth athlete's running stride to reach that adobe corner. He perceived that she had passed through the alley safely, and emerged into the vague light of an open lot. He paced through the narrow odorous passage, careful not to kick tin cans and bottles lying amid the rubbish.

Halfway across the vacant rubble-heaped lot, the dark quick form of a man sprang from the shadow of mulberry and pecan trees, pounced on the woman, hand clasped to her mouth before she could scream, flung her to the ground and piled savagely on top of her. Travers pulled his Colt and sprinted forward with flowing speed. Trav clutched the man's throat, hauled him back off the girl, and jerked him upright. Travers's explosive strength had surprised many a border ruffian.

"I oughta shoot your head off, you sonofabitch," Travers said, soft but with deadly intensity, spinning the man about to face him. "Get your hands up."

The young Mexican raised his hands and clasped them behind his neck. "Don't shoot!" he panted. "I got no gun. I meant no harm. I love this woman."

Travers's eyes swerved to the girl, who had scrambled to her feet and was brushing off her torn dress. "I never saw him before."

"You want me to shoot him?"

She shrugged. "If you don't, he'll try it again. With me or somebody else, Juarez won't miss one more rapist."

"I think I'll just beat him half to death." Travers sheathed his gun.

"Look out!" the girl screamed.

The Mexican's right hand flashed forward and a steel blade streaked at Travers's chest. He had caught a warning in those fiery eyes, even before the girl cried out, and Trav twisted aside and drew in one swift sinuous motion, the .44 jolting his wrist as burnt-orange flame stabbed into the Mex's body and sent him reeling backward to land flat on his shoulders, writhing and squirming. No second shot was necessary. The man was dead.

"You're pretty good with that gun," the girl said.

"It's my business to be."

"You don't look like a gunfighter. But you're sure fast enough."

Travers smiled thinly at her. "You shouldn't be walking around alone at night. You oughta know better."

"I do." She laughed lightly. "But a girl's not safe anywhere these days, I guess." She was readjusting the flower in her hair.

"Especially a girl like you," Travers drawled.

"What do you mean by that?"

"You know what I mean. An attractive girl."

She pouted childishly. "Attractive? Most men call me beautiful."

"I'm a master of understatement."

"What? Oh, I get it. You're a very smart boy."

"I'll walk you home," Travers said, closing the loading gate after replacing the spent cartridge.

"You don't need to. I live right over there."

Travers took her arm. "I will anyway. Did he hurt you?"

"Just my feelings. I want to thank you for—for saving me, Mister—?"

"Travers. It was a pleasure. What's your name?"

"Rosita. Rosita Shaw."

Mex mother, Yank father, thought Travers. Quite a gal. "You should stay off the streets at night. Isn't there somebody—anybody who cares?"

Her smile was wistful. "No, not really. I'm alone. Of course I live with another girl, a little older and wiser than me. I drive her crazy."

"I can imagine." They were walking together in easy unison.

"I'm not a bad girl though. I just like to fool around and have fun."

"That's dangerous. You're asking for trouble."

"Everything's dangerous on the Rio Grande," Rosita Shaw said, arching her brilliant eyes up at him. "You're awful good-looking, Travers. You act as if you don't know it. I'll bet that's part of your charm. Is Travers your first name or last?"

"Last. They call me Trav, mostly."

"I like that. I know you well enough to call you Trav, don't I? You saved my life—or at least my virtue. You saved me from a fate worse than death, they call it in books."

Travers laughed softly. The feminine fragrance of her filled his nostrils and stirred his blood. "It was nothing, Rosita. Forget it."

"Nothing to you maybe. Mighty important to me, Trav. If I was a man I'd be a gunfighter. Like you, Trav. A gunfighter who looked like Prince Charming." Her voice was shaky now, her laugh a trifle hysterical. The delayed reaction was setting in. Rosita Shaw had been too calm and cool, at first. "That man's name is Reboza, I think, one of Hook Cano's killers."

Travers drew her close under his left arm, meaning to comfort and reassure her. He felt the lush warmth of her breast and hip, pressing against him as they walked, and the rising flicker of desire deep in his groin.

"I thought Hook Cano was the handsomest devil in the world," Rosita murmured. "He can't hold a candle to you, Trav."

"You *know* Hook Cano?" He was astonished.

"I *knew* him, I was his girl once. That's why I'm safe from most men in most places. They think I may still be Hook's woman, and they're afraid. But that's all over. He found a woman he liked better, and I was gone, out in the cold."

"You know where he lives now, Rosita?"

"Nobody seems to know that, Trav. I couldn't love him anymore anyway. I've heard too many terrible things about him. Couldn't believe them at first, but now I know they're all true." She shuddered. "He's a wicked man. I hope they catch him and hang him."

Travers was silent and preoccupied. They had crossed the street at the far end of the open lot, and Rosita Shaw gestured at a small square adobe with window shades outlined by lemon strips of light. "That's where I live, Trav. Looks like Nora's home. Won't you come in and have a drink?"

"I'd like to, Rosita, but I have to meet some people," he lied. He wanted this girl, but he'd resolved not to take her, for some reason he could not fathom. It was sense-less to pass up such an opportunity. He'd already grown old enough to regret many of the lovely women he might have possessed—and did not. He'd begun to com-prehend that his very first girl, Priscilla Cabot, was the one he loved and wanted always.

"Will I see you again, Trav?" asked Rosita.

"Yeah, if I stay in El Paso, I'll come to see you, baby."

"What do you do, Trav?"

"I'm a Ranger."

"Oh God, oh no!" she cried. "If you're a Ranger, you won't live long enough to see me again. I heard tonight in the Sierra that Captain Rube Caldwell was dead."

"I don't believe that, Rosita."

"I don't know, Trav. But they said he shot himself in the head. The last Ranger left in El Paso—until you came."

"Now I know it's just a false rumor," Travers de-clared. "Rube would never do that. No matter how hopeless things were. He'd never kill himself."

"Please come in, Trav," pleaded Rosita. "Now that it's all over, I'm getting scared and sick, shaking all over."

"Sorry, baby, but I have to go. I do have an appoint-ment—business. I will come back though."

"The place isn't good enough for you," Rosita ac-cused, abjectly.

"Of course it is. Don't ever think that way about me.

I just can't afford to miss this meeting."

"You don't want me because I admitted to being Hook Cano's girl—years and years ago."

"It's not that either. I do want you, Rosita. I'll be back and prove it, very soon."

Rosita bent her dark glinting head. "I have my own room in there, you know. We'd be all alone together, real private. Don't leave me, Trav, I need you so. I want to love you, thank you with all I've got, honey."

"Not tonight, babe," Travers said gently. "It can't be done. But we'll be together before long."

A wind came up in the night, blowing dirt, sand, and specks of snow along the empty street. Most of the houses were dark now, smoke spiraling up from the chimneys. The moon and stars were clouded over, the gusty air growing colder. Somewhere dogs barked, cows mooed, and coyotes cried into the blackness. Mission bells chimed and bare branches rustled dryly.

Rosita Shaw shivered and swayed against Travers, her strong young arms gripping, breasts and belly crushed to him, her sweet face lifted to meet his kiss. His arms went around her with tender power, and wildfire coursed in their blood. Their mouths clung, their tongues mingled, and there was nothing but their fierce need for one another. Suddenly Travers felt young and wild, gay, daring and devil-may-care, a reckless boy again.

"To hell with that meeting," he said, against her lips.

"Oh, my darling, my dearest one!" Rosita Shaw cried, and led him eagerly, joyously, to the door of the little adobe house.

NINE

The funeral was a big one, attended by all the local dignitaries, officials, and prominent business men, as well as the real friends and acquaintances Rube Caldwell had accumulated over the years: ordinary citizens, townspeople, ranchers, cowboys, storekeepers, bartenders, stable hands, gunsmiths, saddle-makers, lawmen, blacksmiths, soldiers, and town loafers.

The three Rangers—Edley, Travers and Bouchard—dressed in clean pressed dark suits, white shirts, black string ties, and saddle-soaped boots, served as bearers, along with three officers from the Border Patrol. Travers had been asked to deliver the eulogy. He agreed to write it, but said he was no public speaker. Trav did write it, Judge Milo Bascomb orated, and it was a beautiful tribute to Rube Caldwell.

Susan Caldwell, gowned in severe black with a heavy veil, conducted herself with simple dignity and composure. The three children, two boys and a girl, were too young to understand death, but they knew their father was gone, and wouldn't be coming back. In the past year or so, Rube had been away most of the time anyway, so the kids weren't as lonely as they might have been.

After the graveside ceremony and burial, the Rangers

accompanied Susan and the children home. Susan had no relatives or close friends among her neighbors, and neither had Rube, although acquaintances had brought all kinds of food and delicacies to the house. Fox Edley showed his partners the office, and explained how everything had been locked and barred from the inside.

"I still can't believe it, Fox," said Milt Travers.

"Me neither," Rusty Bouchard grumped. "It wasn't Rube's way, nohow."

"I feel the same way," Fox Edley said. "But all the facts point to suicide. You gotta admit that."

While Susan prepared lunch for the children, the men went out to the barn beyond the walled patio to care for the livestock. There were two horses, a milch cow, a large friendly dog and an aloof cat, chickens and a rooster.

"With Rube gone all the time, Susan must have had to tend to these animals, as well as the kids," Bouchard said.

"No, Rube hired a man for these chores, Sue told me," said Edley. "His black stallion's downtown at the livery stable."

They were hard hit by Caldwell's death, and full of sympathy for the widow and children, but Susan was cold and distant, her gracious warmth and cheerful pleasantry gone. The Rangers felt obligated to stay with her, although she didn't make them feel welcome or wanted. A woman shouldn't be left alone at a time like this. They were most comfortable when drinking, and in this department Susan joined them, drink for drink, handling the booze as well as the men did.

When they returned from the barnyard tasks, the children had been put to bed for their naps, and Susan was drinking alone in the parlor. She needed women friends around, but there didn't seem to be any. Lily Lavoy could be a great help to her, Bouchard thought, but knew that Susan would not tolerate Lily's presence. It was a shame, because Lily could have done so much for the bereaved lady. But women were queer, unpredictable critters at best. They seldom liked one another.

The conversation was disjointed and desultory, the participants groping from one topic to another without much incentive. The atmosphere was morbid and depressing. If not a public orator, Travers could generally handle private situations with tact and finesse, but today he seemed tongue-tied. Edley was struck dumb by Susan's attitude, and Bouchard's well of humorous anecdotes had dried up. Susan was still in a state of shock.

The inner thoughts of the Rangers tended to follow the same somber trend. A man, a fine man, had spent about a decade of his life in this house. He had brought his lovely bride here, fathered three children, worked hard and long without letup, experienced emotions from the heights of happiness to the depths of desolation. Now he was gone, those ten years wiped out, as if he had never lived here at all, never even been here. It made everything seem hopeless, worthless, an empty travesty, a cruel fantasy. A man's life snuffed out like a candle, and nothing left.

Susan's next words startled them: "You never knew Rube was a ladies' man, did you? Not even you, Foxcroft, who knew him best. Well, he turned into one. He had a woman here in El Paso." Her laugh was brittle as glass. "Her name is Lily Lavoy."

Fox Edley laughed outright, and the other two men smiled, as if in relief.

"They were just friends, Susie," said the Fox. "We're all friends of Lily Lavoy. It doesn't mean a thing."

"He was sleeping with her," Susan stated flatly. "Been sleeping with her for years. I *know* that, for a fact.

The great whore of the Rio Grande, and my husband was in love with her."

"No, Susan," Bouchard said gruffly. "Lily flirts and kids around with all of us, but that's all. She don't have affairs."

"She probably goes to bed with all of you, too. But that doesn't alter the fact that she had an affair with Rube, and he really loved her. Far more than he did his wife and children."

Travers shook his tawny head solemnly. "No Susan. That was nothing but gossip and evil rumors. Rube wasn't that kind of a man—even before he married you."

She laughed a trifle wildly. "Perhaps I drove him to it, then. Come on, boys. Your glasses are empty. Fill 'em up and drink 'em down!"

The cattle and horses herded into the stockyards, the Anvil group and Lashtrow went to the Hotel Pueblo, which was cheaper and nearer the yards than the Franklin. Two night watchmen with rifles and revolvers presided over the pens, but they would offer little opposition if the raiders struck from across the river.

"Is Rube Caldwell in town?" Lash asked the desk clerk.

"The Ranger captain?" The man gave him a strange startled look. "He's dead, mister, dead and buried."

"Dead?" Lashtrow stared incredulously. "Who killed him?"

"They say he killed himself. Sorry to have to tell yuh like this."

"Rube Caldwell? Don't you ever believe that."

The clerk smiled wanly under his drooping mustache. "I never did, mister. But they're callin it suicide. He was buried today."

Lashtrow excused himself from the Ashley party

which was just coming in after unsaddling their broncs and unhitching the mules. Lash had left his sorrel saddled and at the rack out front. The Anvil riders were anxious to get washed up and out on the town, and Ash and Amanda were ready for supper and bed. He didn't tell them about Rube; they'd hear it soon enough.

Numb and hollow, Lashtrow strode out, down the steps, and climbed back into the saddle. There was little traffic in the streets. He rode for the Franklin Hotel at the center of the community, booting the sorrel into a high lope. Rube must be dead, but Lash couldn't believe it was by his own hand. Somehow the sonsabitches had contrived to make it look like suicide. Another fine man and good Ranger gone, and this one left a wife and three kids. Strong support for Lash's theory that Rangers shouldn't marry. The marriage had been a good sound and happy one, as far as he knew, and poor Susan must be torn apart by grief and loss.

Jonesy was on the desk at the Franklin, a rotund, cherub-faced little man, and he greeted Lashtrow with warmth and respect, after wincing a bit at his trailworn appearance. The Rangers were registered there, but they hadn't been back since the funeral. Jonesy voiced his sympathy and condolences, asking Lash to relay them to Mrs. Caldwell. It was a terrible blow to El Paso and all Texas, losing a man like Rube Caldwell.

In the passage to the hotel bar, Lash realized what a disreputable figure he must be, unshaven, filthy, ragged from the trail drive, twin Colts packed under his dirty cord jacket. But what the hell difference did it make? Rube Caldwell was dead. Nothing else mattered at the moment.

The saloon was smoky under the grand chandeliers, and a feminine voice called, "Lash!" He turned and saw Lily Lavoy sitting alone at her secluded alcove table. She stood up to embrace and kiss him, as she had Bouchard. "Sit down, please." She indicated the brandy bottle and extra glass. "I've been waiting and hoping to see you, Lash." Her eyes were reddened from weeping. "I couldn't even go to the funeral, goddamn it! I was the best friend Rube had in this town."

Lily needed no rouge to color her cheeks or enhance her ripe red lips. She was brimming with vitality that no amount of debauchery seemed to dim. Other females lied when they said Lily's hair was bleached and dyed. It was as natural a golden blonde as her eyes were jade green under naturally long curling lashes. Her fullblown figure was as breath-taking as ever. Lily Lavoy was a beauty. Hard and brazen and doomed, perhaps, but lovely to look at.

"You've been a good friend to all of us, Lily," Lash told her.

"It was special with Rube." She poured more brandy into his glass. "The nearest to love I'll ever know, Lash."

"I didn't know that, Lil." Lash was truly surprised.

"Well, that's the way it was. And Rube loved me, too. Of course he'd never leave his wife and family for a scarlet woman. I didn't want him to. . . . Do you think he killed himself?"

"No, I can't believe that."

"Neither can I, Lash. He was murdered, and it was arranged to look like suicide. I'm sure of that."

"I don't know any of the details," Lashtrow said. "I just got in, haven't seen the boys or anyone."

"Did you save the Ashleys?"

Lash slowly shook his head. "Not their ranch. It was burned before we got there. The Ashleys and their crew are all right, and we drove the herd down here."

Lily Lavoy was quick. "They let you make the drive,

so they could steal the herd after it got here."

"I'm afraid that's their plan," he admitted.

"Where's your partner? Was it Rammel?"

Lashtrow nodded, light glossing his bronze head. "The Ashley girl, Donna, was sick in Pinon. Ram stayed up there to bring her down when she's well enough."

"I can't really think of anything but Rube, Lash."

"Neither can I, Lily."

"You're going up to the house, I suppose. The other boys are still there." Lily tossed off her drink, and refilled both glasses. "I feel sorry for Susan and the kids. I wish I could go there and help, but of course it's out of the question. It's awful to be shut outside, when someone you love dies."

"I know, Lil, I know." His large brown hand covered her dainty white one on the tabletop. "We'll get together —later."

"Did it ever occur to you that Susan Caldwell might have a lover?"

"No, Lil, it never did," said Lashtrow. "Never considered such a thing."

"She has, Lash. I'm sure she has," Lily declared.

Lashtrow sat silent, disbelieving.

"Of course, you won't believe a nice high-class lady like Susan could do such a thing!" Lily Lavoy flared. "It's only the dance-hall doxies like me who ever do wrong, isn't it, Lash?"

"Please, Lil, don't be like that. I'm not that stupid about women. Did Rube know about it? Or suspect anything?"

"I don't think so. He never mentioned it anyway."

"If it was true and he knew of it, it might have led him to kill himself."

"*Nothing* could've made Rube Caldwell kill himself," Lily said, with positive finality. "Nothing in God's world, Lash."

"I think you're right there, Lil," agreed Lashtrow, raising his glass to click against hers. "Here's to him, one of the best." They drank together, and Lash went on, "I'd better get out to the house now. Be brave, sweet lady. We'll all see you soon."

"Take care of yourself, Lash." She watched him walk back to the corridor leading to the lobby, a big man moving with easy grace.

Lily poured herself another and slumped back in her chair, feeling alone and friendless. She sensed someone staring at her from somewhere, and glanced around the spacious smoke-hazed barroom. In a far corner sat the tall handsome Tatum and the small rodent-like Fasaro, averting their gazes quickly to pretend they were unaware of her presence. But she knew they'd been watching herself and Lash intently.

A sinking sensation of fear turned her cold and ill, hollow and shaken. They had seen her in earnest conversation with Lashtrow, and that might be enough to get her killed. Men like them held human lives cheap, and killed at the slightest provocation. Lily no longer felt immune to danger. She felt frozen through, vulnerable and helpless.

Tiny wind-driven snowflakes laced the premature darkness when Lashtrow left the hotel, and the sorrel had turned its rump to the gusts whipping down from the pass. Blurred lights shone through the turbulence, and ice-like pellets stung Lash's stubbled cheeks and eyelids. He pulled down his hatbrim, tightened the lanyard under his chin, and swung into leather already turned cold.

Riding toward the Caldwell home, he thought of all the dead comrades left along the way, their images flitting one after another through his mind. Montana and his brother, Kid Stick . . . Tonk Hiller, Tess's father, in

Salt Creek . . . Sid Servoss and Swede Nilssen in Old Mexico . . . old Ben Hickey and young Collander up in Nevada . . . tough little Stebbins right here in El Paso . . . And others whose faces and names had faded from memory. And now Rube Caldwell.

The wind ripped at horse and man as they plodded up sloping streets, and the snow thickened and coated them. Lighted windows glowed warm and inviting from the Caldwell house, yet he dreaded going in there. He took the driveway to the barn, and got down to slide the wide door open and lead the sorrel inside. The Rangers' familiar broncs were there: Bouchard's big gray, Travers's coyote dun, and Edley's *grullo,* along with two other horses. Rube's black stud was missing.

Lash unbridled and unsaddled the sorrel, watered him at the trough, draped on a nose-bag of oats, and currycombed the great golden horse thoroughly. It had been a long hard day of trail-driving, and the other riders had switched mounts time and again, but the sorrel seemed tireless as usual.

"Never was a hoss like you, Mate," said Lashtrow lovingly, as he rubbed down the splendid animal. "Never'll be another. You've worn out more hosses than any other bronc that ever lived, Pardner."

Having stalled as long as possible, Lash took a bottle of good sherry out of his saddlebags and started for the house. As he recalled, Susan drank nothing stronger than wine. The snowfall was heavier, steadier, the larger flakes cool and feathery on Lash's gaunted face. The back door was locked so he trudged around to the front.

Fox Edley, trying not to assume too much the man-of-the-house posture, came to open up, his yellow eyes lighting at the sight of Lashtrow. All he said was, "This just about gets you in," as he examined the label on the bottle, and clapped Lash on the shoulder.

Bouchard said, "How, Wolf," using his Osage name.

Lash said, "How, Red Bush."

Anxiety in his blue gaze, Travers asked, "Where's Ram, Lash?"

"He's okay, Trav."

They were all amazed when Susan Caldwell got up and flew into Lashtrow's arms, crying, "Lash, oh Lash," clinging to him, burying her face in his broad chest. "Susan," he murmured, holding her firmly, stroking her dark head tenderly.

Fox Edley thought, She didn't greet me that way, and I was closer to her than Lash. Must be the booze. But not entirely. It was Lashtrow. Without even trying to, Lash seemed to be all things to all women. Some kind of magic about him. They had seen it over and over. Travers called it his "universal charm." Bouchard said he roused the raw animal in them.

"Susan, I'm so goddamn sorry," Lash whispered in her ear. "But you'll get all dirty on me. Didn't know till we got in this afternoon. Didn't stop to clean up. I'm filthy from the trail drive."

"I don't care, Lash," she sobbed quietly. "I'm just glad you're here. I feel better having you here."

They all felt better since his arrival, the whole atmosphere brightened and warmed somehow. Travers had never seen or felt that quality in any other person. He'd endeavored to capture it in his novel, *Men and Guns,* but it was impossible to get it all.

Seated beside Susan, drink in hand, Lashtrow quickly and concisely told them about the foray into New Mexico and the return trip, sketching in a little color and humor to make it more entertaining. They were all loosened up, chatting and laughing pleasantly, when the kids woke and came romping downstairs, greeting everyone politely and then climbing happily all over Uncle Lash.

Jesus Christ, the kids too, thought Fox Edley. Ain't

that the damndest thing though? Lash don't do nothin but be himself, natural as hell, and the whole world changes when he walks into a place.

Later, while Susan got supper for the children, the other men took Lashtrow into the office where the death had occurred. They discussed the case from every angle, and each avenue explored ended at suicide. There was no other solution.

"Unless the killer had an accomplice," Lashtrow said finally. "There had to be more than one involved. A man alone couldn't have done it, unless he was a phantom who passed through brick walls."

"Rube left Susan pretty well fixed financially, I reckon," Fox Edley said. "Made some investments that paid off good, saved his money, owned this house free and clear. There's a will. Everythin goes to Susan and the kids, a course. Except he left me his black stallion. And Lash, he left you a spread he owned outside town."

"There's the ranch you always wanted, Lash," said Milt Travers. "Now you can resign, marry Karen Lindley, and settle down. Take Foxcroft as a partner, put the big black out to stud, raise horses, and run cattle."

Lash regarded him soberly. "I s'pose you're all set to quit the force, marry Priscilla Cabot in Boston, and burn up the literary field?"

Travers shook his princely head sadly. "I plan other's lives much better than my own, I fear, Lash."

Bouchard laughed. "Ram and I may be the last ones left of the Big Five, huh? The youngest and the oldest—and the purtiest."

Lashtrow shaved and scrubbed up in the upstairs washroom, and Travers fetched his warbag for a change of clothing. Trav did the dishes for Susan, while Bouchard and Edley started cooking a meal for the adults. There were beef and pork roasts and hams, vegetables and cakes, pies, cookies, doughnuts, and rolls donated by neighboring families. Red Bush was overjoyed to have such an assortment to ply his culinary arts on. The Fox was an unenthusiastic helper. They exchanged barbed insults as they toiled in the well-equipped kitchen.

Susan had bedded the children for the night, when Lash came downstairs looking like a brand-new man, even though his gray eyes were sunken and his brown cheeks hollowed under the high cheekbones. He needed rest and sleep in the worst way. Susan hugged and kissed him to the point of embarrassment, and Lash was disenchanted by the total change in her. It was painful for Fox Edley to watch, and Lash tried to rebuff her as gently as he could. Never before had they seen her behave in this fashion.

They had an elaborate and festive dinner, and the drinking continued. The Rangers were all astounded at Susan's capacity for liquor. After eating, the exhausted Lashtrow could barely keep his eyes open. It was decided that Lash should sleep in one of the guest rooms on the second floor. Once between pure white sheets he went out like a light. Sometime during the night he came partially awake and heard someone fumbling at the door. It must be Susan. Fortunately the door was bolted securely. He sank back into deep slumber almost instantly.

In the morning the ground was lightly blanketed with snow, and when Lashtrow reached the Yaeger Stockyards they were empty, the Anvil herd and horses gone. Huffnail and Millhauser had not shown up to buy the cattle. They'd been stolen in the night. The worst part of all was that Ashley and his four riders, Arizona and Val Verde, Cobb and Mullen, had crossed the Rio Grande in pursuit of their stock.

TEN

During the big snowstorm in Pinon, New Mexico, the pretty mulatto girl, Melissa, nursed Donna Ashley back to health and sanity, and fought to abstain from drugs herself. Donna's only affliction was from the dope Dr. Keech had pumped into her.

"Thank the Good Lawd he didn't have time to make an addict of her," Melissa told Rammel. "I'm the one that's goin to have trouble. He got me in deep, and I'm goin to need help. I'm tryin to cut down now, but it's hell on earth, Mr. Ram."

Meanwhile Marshal Moncrief, barber Joe Drury, and Rammel labored to get Dr. Ward Bailey sobered and cleaned up enough to resume practicing medicine. The veteran physician responded nobly and recuperated much sooner than they'd dared hope. "Life in the old dog yet," Doc said.

After the blizzard ended and the snow started melting, Dr. Keech's frozen body was buried without ceremony in the local Boothill. Nobody mourned him, and everyone welcomed the return of old Doc Bailey. When no one appeared to claim Keech's property, Moncrief and the town council decreed that Doc Bailey take over the Keech house, office, and small hospital.

Rammel became friendly with Donna Ashley during her convalescence, but he felt no sexual desire for her, alluring as she was, because of her association with Keech. Ram liked her, pitied her, and that was all. He grew even fonder of and more sympathetic to Melissa, seeing her as a helpless victim, whereas Donna had wilfully entered into the relationship with the monstrous Keech. Melissa wanted to seek aid in El Paso, and Rammel agreed to take her along with them. Melissa could ride, and the doctor had given her a pinto pony, the one decent act of his tenure in Pinon. Donna had her own mare in the stable, of course.

Donna Ashley thought Rammel was the most beautiful man she'd ever seen. Six feet tall with light blond hair, green eyes, and a sunny smile, he was slim, graceful, and sharp as a rapier, with courtly manners and a pleasant voice. The hero of all her girlhood dreams and fantasies come to life, Ranger-tough and strong. Emerging from her narcotic haze, she fell instantly in love with him, wondering how she had ever let herself become mesmerized by the repulsive Keech, cursing herself for it. Rammel was kind to her and indulgent, but no more. She'd been used by Keech, and Ram never would want her for himself.

Melissa Johnson too was more than half in love with Rammel, the handsome saviour and gallant, high-bred gentlemen who expected nothing in return. He treated both girls exactly the same, nicely but with cool reserve.

Donna had coppery brown hair, sparkling hazel eyes, a pert roguish face, and a slender supple figure with flowing curves. She knew she was attractive, and Ram would have been interested, had he not known of her shameful affair with Keech.

"You don't like girls much, do you, Ram?" she asked one day.

93

"Sure, I like 'em," Rammel drawled. "But I'm a married man with a baby son."

"I don't believe it," Donna objected outright. "You use that to put off women you don't want to bother with."

"No, it's a fact, Donna." He showed her pictures of Tess and little Travers Rammel. They had made Milt godfather of the child, and Milt had been proud and honored. Lashtrow was disappointed and hurt, but he concealed it well. Ram knew it was there, however.

"Well, I guess that makes you safe enough, Ram," said Donna, with a wry smile.

"I hope so," Rammel said simply.

The town was astonished at the transformation of Marshal Monk Moncrief, a wholly different man since Keech's death. The town fathers were greatly impressed by Rammel, and tried to entice him to settle in Pinon, a few of them hinting at marriage to Donna Ashley, and lucrative business positions.

"I appreciate your interest and consideration," Rammel said. "But I can't desert the Rangers, and I'm already married."

As he and the two girls made ready for the trip to El Paso, Rammel kept expecting somebody to show up and lay claim to Dr. Keech's property. But the days passed, the snow went on melting, and nothing happened. Old Doc Bailey was already back in fulltime practice, which in his case meant a lot of overtime work, too. He was also helping the tortured Melissa stay off drugs, with Donna's assistance. The patient had become a nurse, and vice versa. Rammel also lent a hand to see Melissa through some of the worst withdrawal battles, which were terrifying to witness. Fortunately Melissa was a fighter, determined to break her addiction, all heart and will and courage.

Donna had brought a packhorse from Anvil, along with her saddle horse, and they exercised the animals including Ram's big bay bronco. The girls would require a tent to sleep in, as well as extra blankets, gear, and utensils. Rammel could make out with his bedroll and tarpaulin. The weather was running fair and mild, with only an occasional brief snow squall. The Sacramento peaks were still white, but the slopes and canyons were bare and dry.

They would ride about fifty miles to Orogrande, and catch the stagecoach for El Paso, a distance of some sixty miles more. The trail followed an old wagon road through the southern reaches of the mountain range, not too difficult unless they encountered young bucks broken off a reservation, or a roving band of outlaws. With two young ladies in his care, Rammel didn't care to contemplate those possibilities. Both girls claimed they could shoot, with long and short guns, but they weren't apt to shoot much like Rangers.

Ram often wondered if the Anvil trail herd and its drovers ever reached El Paso. Lashtrow probably overtook them before the storm broke, and he would have gotten them through. Donna said her dad and his four punchers were good fighting men, especially Arizona and Val Verde, the kid gunfighters. Rammel had an immortal faith in Lash, seeing him as invincible. But six men were a small crew to push a thousand or more head through mountain passes in a raging blizzard, and the bandits might have bushwhacked them, too. They might all be dead up there in the Sacramentos, but Ram couldn't believe that of Lash. To him Lash was indomitable, a supreme power, infallible and unbeatable.

Once in a drunken fit of envy and jealousy, Rammel had nearly let Lash die right under his eyes, but another man had busted the backshooter in time. Ram could never forget the sick shame of that moment. Since then, he and Lash had saved one another's lives on numerous occasions. The Big Five were all great with guns, but Lash stood above the rest—far above.

Rammel was running out of money, and it annoyed and angered him. The Rangers weren't overgenerous with expense accounts. Ram was always short, unless riding with Milt Travers—or sometimes Lashtrow. It was a severe annoyance. He'd have to borrow from Moncrief—or Donna Ashley. Either would have made the loan gladly, but Ram hated to ask. Sometimes, for some inexplicable reason, it seemed easier to borrow from women than men. But Ram disliked borrowing money from anyone outside his own group. Until the family fortune dwindled after the Civil War, Ram had taken wealth for granted.

Born and raised in luxury and grandeur on a plantation outside of Culpeper, Virginia, the Rammel children had never expected to lack for riches. By the fortunes of war, the Travers family had retained its financial dynasty in Louisburg Square, Boston. Bouchard came from a middling poor family in Bristol, Connecticut, but had been on the frontier since his teens. Fox Edley's first home was a saloon in Rock River, Wyoming. Only Lashtrow was a native Texan, from a small family spread near Uvalde.

An odd heterogeneous collection from widely scattered points around the country, with natures as different as their backgrounds, yet closely united, as men will be when they have faced death together.

On this winter afternoon under a low pewter sky, Rammel had taken his bay gelding out for a good run. He was lonely for Tess and the baby, and eager to rejoin his friends in El Paso. Melissa was fit enough now, and they were starting the long trek tomorrow. Financial pressure weighed on him.

Back in town he saw Marshal Moncrief's red roan at the tie-rail in front of the Mescalero Saloon. Rammel dismounted, and tossed his reins over the rack. The stormdoor was open and he elbowed through the broken-slatted swing doors. Moncrief was the sole drinker at the bar, with a quiet poker game in progress at a rear corner table. The marshal's cold rocky features warmed as he saw Ram, and he poured whisky from his bottle into another clean glass and paid for the beer Ram ordered.

"Sure goin ta miss yuh, pard."

"Monk, I may have to borrow a little money to pay my livery bill and make the trip to El Paso." Rammel had been sleeping at the doctor's house, so there was no account to settle at the Otero House.

"Borrow hell!" Moncrief barked with laughter. "I owe you, Ram. I been thinkin you oughta get a bonus for shootin Keech. Got it right here for you. Five hundred bucks." He pressed a sheaf of bills into Ram's pocket.

"I can't take that, Monk. I don't need that much."

"By the jeezus, you're goin to take it!" Moncrief insisted. "It's Keech's money, so what the hell? Oughta be a lot more." His stony face and slate eyes hardened. "Them jaspers finally got here to claim Keech's place. A fat squatty Mex named Vargas and a mule-faced white called Stokes. They look like gunnies to me, up from the border."

"They pretending to be relatives or what?" asked Rammel, chasing his whisky with beer.

"Naw, they got legal documents provin Keech was a pardner in the Livestock and Land Syndicate, or some such damn thing. Havin no next-of-kin, everythin Keech had was to go to the syndicate in El Paso. It's all notarized and signed by Keech, Judge Bascomb, Mayor Amos Essling, and Sheriff Kriewold. Looks legal as hell. Our lawyer O'Brien is goin through it now."

"Fakers," Rammel said, in mild scorn. "The whole thing's trumped up. Everyone says those signers are stealing El Paso blind. They sent up two hired guns—or perhaps a pair of Hook Cano's *pistoleros*. Where are they, Monk?"

"Lookin over the doctor's place. Prob'ly throwin out Doc Bailey and the two gals. We better ramble over there, Ram."

"Let's go." They downed their drinks, Moncrief took his bottle, and they walked out of the saloon to mount up and ride, unhurriedly.

On horseback, Rammel said, "If they make a fight of it, Monk, try to take one of 'em alive. Might clear up some things in El Paso for us."

"You sure they're crooked, Ram?" queried Moncrief, uncertainly.

"Dead sure," Rammel said. "The names of Bascomb, Essling, and Kriewold guarantee that. They're part of the vipers' nest we've got to clean out."

Approaching the yellow-painted frame house, they heard the muffled scream of a woman and put spurs to their mounts. "Take the back, Monk," said Rammel. "I'll go in the front." He was keened to a steel edge for combat, strung taut but moving loosely, a hollow thrumming in his chest.

The front door was unlocked. Rammel went in through the entry-hall, slipped through the heavy yellow drapes, gun in hand, and burst into the doctor's office.

A medium-sized white man with a blunt dour visage and black goatee was holding a pistol to Dr. Ward Bailey's tousled silvery head. The physician was seated stiffly in a straight-backed chair.

"Drop it or you're dead," Rammel said.

"The hell you say." Stokes brayed like a mule. "*You* drop it, or *he's* dead."

"You'll go a split-second after him."

Stokes shrugged slightly. He was a gunman all right, cold as ice, his left hand on Bailey's collar. "Might use the doc here as a shield. Who the hell are you anyway?"

"I'm a Ranger." Ram's voice was calmer than he felt inside.

Another bray from Stokes. "That don't mean shit up here, kid."

"This iron does," Rammel said, green eyes steady on his adversary, but with peripheral vision watching Moncrief slip silently in through an open side door, his .45 poised.

"You ain't got the time, sonny," Stokes said, dead-panned and flat-toned. "The old man here's lived long enough. You don't mind dyin, do you, Doc?"

"Not as long as you die, too," Ward Bailey said, emotionless.

"He's got a lotta guts, I'll give him that." Stokes tightened his left hand in Bailey's collar, ready to blow off his head and swing his body from the chair to catch Rammel's bullet.

"You'll never make it," Rammel warned him, as Moncrief crept closer.

"For chrisake, punk! I was killin men before you was born."

"You've been at it too long, mule-face. It's time you folded."

"Okay, pretty boy," Stokes said. "Here goes the doc's head."

Moncrief took one more stride and struck viciously with the long gun barrel. Stokes's hatted head sank low under the crushing impact, and he collapsed forward against Bailey, rolled off and pitched to the floor in a senseless sprawl. The doctor slid sideways from the chair and stood upright, trembling all over but undaunted. "I'm obliged to you boys."

Another scream floated down the stairwell, and Rammel spun out the doorway and up the staircase, three steps at a time, slamming in through the bedroom door from which the noises issued. The scene might have been ludicrous on the stage, or in other situations. An old melodrama.

Donna and Melissa, their clothes all but torn off them, cowered back on the bed, eyes wide with horror. The fat little Mex, Vargas, held a revolver on them and had just dropped his pants to his ankles, revealing a suit of red-flannel underwear. Attempting to kick free of the binding trousers, he twisted about and fired wildly. Ram felt the hot blinding concussion that blew the hat off his fair head, and shifted so he wouldn't be firing toward the women. He squeezed the trigger.

Vargas tripped in his ankle-tangled pants, and fell headlong as Ram's first bullet passed over him. Vargas fired again from the floor, and shattered a window behind the Ranger. Rammel shot him twice, through the chest and throat. Blood fountained into the gunsmoke and Vargas twitched into a final stillness. Ram made a sweeping outward gesture, and the girls fled sobbing from the fuming room. "Son of a bitch," he said softly.

Rammel recovered his hat and stared numbly at the bullet holes. That had been close, godawful close. Sheer luck or the top of his skull would have gone with the hat. Later they would laugh at the episode, highlighted by the red-flannel underwear of the squat ugly Mexican, but right now it was no laughing matter. Mechanically he reloaded and left the powder-reeking bedroom, void of feeling. The fear would come later.

The girls had donned robes to cover their near-na-
kedness and were waiting in the second-floor hallway,
not prostrated as Ram had visualized them. "Is Doc
Bailey all right?" was their first mutual question.

Rammel nodded dully. "He's fine. You girls better
come down and have some brandy."

"Is the other one dead, too?" Donna Ashley inquired.

"No, Monk just knocked him out."

"Thank God you aren't hurt, Ram!" said Donna,
with deepest feeling.

"A-men," drawled Rammel.

ELEVEN

Lashtrow packed his saddlebags with staple provisions, extra .44–49 ammunition which fitted both long and handguns, cigars and whisky. *Why couldn't they have waited?* he thought. *Goddamn it, they shoulda waited.* Yet he comprehended how the fury of Ashley and his men made it impossible for them to wait, after having their ranch burned and then their stock stolen. Knowing the rustlers had let Anvil trail-drive the herd through the mountains, so all they'd have to do was clear out the stockyards and run the cattle across the border. Enough to madden a saint.

Lash left his horse in the stable. Even the superb sorrel needed rest before another long campaign. Selecting a hammer-headed rawboned mustang of indefinite color, Lash threw on and cinched tight his saddle and gear. The livery man was more than satisfied to have the sorrel as guarantee of payment for rental of the ugly bronc. At the Hotel Pueblo, Lash said goodby to Amanda Ashley, a distraught but courageous woman, and asked her to please call the Rangers at the Franklin, tell them what had happened, and relay his order for them to stay in El Paso. The boys wouldn't like it, but they'd realize the wisdom of it—he hoped.

It was simple enough to follow the wide trampled course of the herd, out past winter-blighted cornfields and vineyards, and over muddy *acequias,* to a shallow ford downstream in the Rio Grande. There was little snow left on the lowlands, except in potholes and wooded areas, but the mountains were still whitecapped and flanked. Mallards winged up raucously from a marsh beside a stand of tamarisk. On the river bluff salt cedars and brown cattails swayed with a brittle sound on the breeze.

The herd had left a broad gouged track down the embankment, and across the shallows the Mexican soil was torn and mashed in similar style. The water flowed cold and murky over the fetlocks of the mustang. On the other bank, hooves churned upward through crushed and mangled reeds, clay mud, and onto foreign ground. He was well below Juarez, Lashtrow noticed, as he took a look back at the mountain portal of El Paso, and the trail led southwest toward the massed peaks of the Sierra Madre. He pushed the gelding into a strong steady gait, wanting to overtake the Anvil riders before they were ambushed and massacred. The *bandidos* might not expect to be pursued into Old Mexico; that was one thing in the Americans' favor.

Lashtrow cantered over barren stony wastes studded with gray granjeno thickets and frayed sachahuiste clusters, past buttes shaped like broken brownstone houses or gothic-spired cathedrals. There was always a different feeling on this side, a sense of ancient evil, hatred, and violence. As many times as Lash had invaded this country, he was still aware of that change in atmosphere once the river was crossed. Mainly in the mind perhaps, but nonetheless deep and irrefutable.

The herd was eight or nine hours ahead of him, Lash estimated, but the tracks of the pursuers he picked out here and there were much fresher. He should catch up to them this afternoon; they only had an hour or so head-start. By taking to higher, rougher terrain at intervals, Lash could cut down the distance. He figured a score of *caballeros* was hazing the cattle along. Then he came to a spot where a bunch, maybe half that number, had doubled back into the north toward Juarez. The big ones, no doubt—Tatum, Fasaro, Quadah, Pablito, possibly Hook Cano himself. Too important to waste time on a trail drive. The stock had gone on in the direction of the mountains, the great mother range of Mexico. The spoor was increasingly fresher.

Lash wondered why he hadn't seen the dust of the detachment that headed homeward, but they'd likely gone to some village for rest and refreshment. There were tiny settlements here and there in the vast waste-lands. Ahead of him now he spotted traces of dust, and spurred the mustang into a swifter pace. The brute had speed and stamina to spare.

The gusty air was sharp but not cold enough to bite. Lashtrow drank from his canteen, took a fresh chew, and rode on in comfort, his winter jacket open. There was no snow here, except on the distant mountains. In early afternoon he caught sight of the Anvil crew, halted to rest in the shelter of a reddish yellow mesa, and smiled in relief as he identified all five, safe and intact. The lank Ashley, burly Cobb, compact Mullen, whiplike Arizona, and little Val Verde. They were starting on-ward when Lash fired a shot skyward to stop them, and rode forward grinning. They greeted him with profane pleasure, as he joined them.

"Ash, you shoulda waited," Lashtrow said gently. "But I know how you felt."

"Couldn't wait for nobody or nothin," the rancher said. "Never been so goddamn mad in all my life." His eyes were bitter in his thin tired face.

"Was about twenty a the bastards, but they split up," Cobb said, his full round visage grim, heavy jaws knotted with muscle.

"Only left about eight with the herd." Arizona laughed with reckless gaiety. "They won't give us much trouble."

"They never thought we'd cross the river," Val Verde chirped. "The christly fools."

"Goin to be some surprised greasers." A homely grin split Mullen's rough red features. "Mighty pleased to see yuh, Lash."

Ashley turned somber. "Was that true, Lash, about Rube Caldwell?"

"Yeah, he's dead, Ash," said Lashtrow sadly.

"Didn't kill himself though, did he?" Ashley was perplexed.

"Looks like he did. But we still got our doubts," Lash drawled.

"I knew Rube pritty well," Ashley muttered. "Can't see him doin that."

Arizona gestured impatiently. "Let's ride. We can catch them sonsabitches before dark."

"Gits dark damn early these days," Val Verde reminded him.

"So what, Val? I got night-rider's eyes, yuh know."

"You got more shit than a goose, Arizona," said Val Verde, with a sour grin, and Arizona's laughter floated musically on the wind.

They rode on at a brisk trot, the broncs frisky in spite of the miles. Sandhills rolled monotonously away on all sides, patched with mesquite and agrito, and canyons gashed the rocky landscape. Creeks and waterholes were marked by willows and green jarillo. The Sierra Madre loomed in stark serrated grandeur on the southwestern horizon, dark, mysterious, and threatening. The border wasn't that far behind, but they had the sense of being deep in enemy territory.

Lashtrow wondered what had become of Caldwell's three Rangers. He hardly expected to see them alive again—or even dead. In the last few years a dozen Rangers had vanished in this country, having been lured across the line and murdered by Cano's gang, without a doubt. That dashing, hook-handed sonofabitch had a lot to answer for. Lash had seen him a few times, but not in recent years. A handsome, swaggering, devil-may-care man with brilliant eyes and a dazzling smile, a steel hook for a right hand, and lightning-fast with his left hand, it was said. Of late he'd become damn near invisible. His name was heard everywhere, but Hook Cano was seldom seen in public.

The signs of the herd freshened in front of them. It looked as if they might catch up with the rustlers before nightfall. Lash hoped they would not encounter any other bands with eyes on the herd. There were still Apaches and Comanches around, fugitives from the reservations. Not as powerful and menacing as in the past, but still capable of launching occasional bloody raids on either side of the border.

Then with stunning suddenness the weather changed. The wind rose to wicked velocity, dark clouds scudded overhead to blot out the pallid sun, and with the chilling cold and blackness came sleet, hail, and snow. The horsemen had to forget the cattle and seek cover for themselves, find shelter somewhere and strive to live through the storm.

By sheer good fortune they blundered into the littered yard of an isolated adobe homestead, where a kindly, warm-hearted Mexican family welcomed them in from the gale-force blizzard. There was a stout barn large enough for the horses, and the solid adobe-brick house proved spacious enough to accommodate six extra men.

There was a potbelly stove, a cook stove, and crude wide fireplace, with plenty of wood stacked in corners. The heat was delightful. A small, nearly black man, a huge fat almost white woman, and three teenage children comprised the family. The man offered tequila, apologizing for it and the poorness of his home, but they bade him save it, producing their own liquor from saddlebags. They all drank together. The woman ladled chili from an iron pot into polished wooden bowls for them, and the kids sat back staring with wide white eyes in shy dark faces. The big gringos were from another world.

Later, the Mexican got out his guitar to accompany his wife, who sang Spanish love songs with amazing clarity and sweetness. It was cheery and comfortable in the ruddy firelight, with the storm howling and raging outside the thick mud-brick walls. The host and hostess were overjoyed when Val Verde took the guitar and Arizona rendered some songs of his own, in a fine tuneful baritone. The Mex couple chattered happily, while Lashtrow and Ashley lounged back on their bedrolls, watching and drinking whisky. Cobb and Mullen remained at the table, beating time with their rope-scarred fists, saluting the musicians with frequent toasts.

It was a gala evening, when they could have been freezing to death outside in that blizzard.

Fate is quite a joker, Lashtrow mused. Here in the land of the enemy, we stumble from certain death into a haven of warmth and security, and are treated with a hospitality that tugs at the heart. Señor and Señora Potasi, the salt of the earth. The poor of any race were the best-hearted. They had very little, but what there was they shared freely.

"Jeezus," Ashley murmured beside him. "They could lose the whole herd in a blizzard like this."

"They know the country," Lash said, with more confidence than he felt. "They'll get the stock into a high-walled canyon, where they can survive, Ash."

If the storm continued, all traces of the herd would be obliterated. They'd been headed toward Galeana, on the Rio de Ste. Maria, and the Rangers had a friend there, good old Chappy. The drive might bypass the town, but Chiapas would know where they were going. Without leaving his cantina, Chappy knew about everything that went on in the vicinity. He had aided the Rangers before, and he would again. He held Lash and his comrades in high esteem. That was the only consoling thought that occurred to Lash tonight.

Lashtrow deliberated on the safety of Susan Caldwell in El Paso. The Ranger trio, Fox Edley in particular, would see to her safety. Lily Lavoy might be in danger. She was known to have been intimate with Rube Caldwell, and some Cano spy could have observed her in long serious conversation with Lash in the Franklin Hotel saloon. Rusty Bouchard would keep an eye on her. And Milt Travers would maintain close observation of the moguls in city hall. But no one could be considered really safe in that town, until the syndicate and Hook Cano's outfit were busted and rubbed out of existence.

If this storm hadn't broken, they'd be driving the Anvil herd homeward tomorrow. Now it would take several days, at least, maybe an entire week. But what the hell, we're lucky to be alive, Lashtrow told himself. Count your blessings, boy, and be grateful.

The steady roar and racket of the blizzard had slackened considerably. Señor Potasi came back from the outhouse behind the house, and said it still snowed a little but not much. The winds were dying down; the worst was over. He told the two boys and girl to go to bed in their tiny cubicles back of the kitchen.

Soon it was time for all hands to retire, drowsy from the heat and liquor. Señora Potasi was sad to have the fiesta end, and said the visitors had brought them happiness from out of the storm.

Arizona bowed low to her. "Señora, you sing beautifully, your chili is the finest, and we are deeply in your debt. It has been a night to remember."

"*Gracias,* señor." She smiled at them all, her large dark eyes shining wetly.

"We have a good time," Potasi said. "This room is yours for the night. Be at home in it and sleep well. The privy is close by behind the house." He and his wife withdrew to their bedroom.

The men had another round of drinks, arranged their blankets with jackets for pillows, and one after another went outside to relieve their kidneys. Lash went last. The night air was calm, the snow falling softly in scattered flakes. A few stars sparkled clear of the thinning clouds, and then a white moon sailed radiantly free of cover. It was close to the full, Lash thought. It'd help when they caught up with the herd.

Lashtrow hoped Rammel and the Ashley girl, Donna, were doing all right. They ought to be reaching El Paso before long. Lash looked up at the moon. Don't let Ram fall for the girl. It was a silent prayer. Tess has got troubles enough without that.

Lash returned to the interior. It was almost too hot now. The lamps had been turned off, and the only light came from scarlet and gold embers in the fireplace. The others were stretched loosely in their blankets on the beaten earth floor. Lash said, "Good night, boys," and there was a sleepy chorus of responses. The main front room smelled of spicy foods, whisky, wood- and tobacco-smoke. Lashtrow thought of Karen Lindley with a pang of desire and loneliness. At times the want and need for her were painful, almost unbearable. But this was no way to get to sleep. He tried to think of nothing, but her lovely vision persisted.

He muffled a groan with his arm across his mouth.

In the morning the land was white as far as a man could see in every direction, with nothing to show that a herd of over a thousand had ever passed this way. Dazzling, unbroken white, after the pink of the rising sun paled away. A pretty sight if you weren't on the trail of some rustlers.

Ashley looked at Lashtrow with an expression of baffled despair, bitter and hopeless. Whipthong tough at fifty, he was weary and depressed.

"Don't worry, Ash." He placed a reassuring hand on the rancher's thin, bony shoulder. "They were pointing for Galeana. I have a good friend there who'll know where the herd went. We'll find 'em all right."

"How far to Galeana?" asked Ashley.

"Maybe a hundred twenty miles."

Ashley moaned. "Maybe they never got that far, Lash."

"If they didn't, we'll find 'em on the way."

"Sure we'll find 'em, boss." Mullen stroked his bristled red cheek. "No goddamn way we ain't goin to find them dogies."

"If we don't I'm ruined," Ashley mumbled. "Just plain and complete goddamn ruined, my whole life down the drain."

"Don't fret, Ash." Arizona smiled brightly at him. "Hell ain't deep or far enough for 'em to hide them cattle."

"Dead sure right," Val Verde drawled dourly. "Arizona'd bring 'em back all by himself, you just give him the word."

TWELVE

Lily Lavoy's suite of rooms occupied the entire second floor above a dry-goods shop on Curtice Street, just off the central plaza in El Paso. Gregarious and fun-loving as she was, Lily liked and needed privacy. Her home was a well-kept secret. She never entertained there, except in the case of someone like Rube Caldwell or Rusty Bouchard or a rare woman friend. Few people had any idea where she lived. Most assumed she had a permanent room in the Franklin Hotel. She was always in the bar there.

The second floor had been renovated under Lily's explicit directions. The rooms were lavishly overfurnished, with deep-piled Persian and Turkish rugs, velvet-cushioned chairs and divans, carved tables, and walls agleam with gold-framed mirrors, silver-framed pictures, colorful tapestries and drapes, shelves of knick-knacks. The living room had a broad fieldstone fireplace, an ample well-filled bookcase, and mirrors everywhere. Lily had a passion for looking-glasses.

There were two entrances. The front stairway was secreted behind an inconspicuous door beside the ornate

111

store entrance. The back outside stairs climbed the adobe wall to a roofed porch, overlooking the shop's loading platform and wagon yard. Upstairs the front door opened into an entry hall, giving access to the chandeliered parlor. Beyond it were opulent bed chambers, a washroom with inside chemical privy, Lily's office or den, a small dining area and large kitchen, with the gallery outside. Unlikely as it seemed, Lily Lavoy loved to cook and experiment with exotic recipes. Whether momentarily rich or nearly broke, she lived in a high fashion. Her closets were crammed with expensive clothes, her jewel boxes glittered with treasures, and her liquor cabinet was always well-stocked.

A cleaning girl came in twice a week to keep the place spotless and shining. Lily paid her generously.

Lily had this day been visited by Rosita Shaw, one of the few women she admitted to her home. The girl was terrified and wanted to borrow money to get out of town and across the border. She had an uncle she could stay with in Old Mexico. He owned a saloon down there.

"I've got to get away, Lil," she said. "They'll kill me if I don't."

"Who'll kill you?" asked Lily. "What the hell happened, Rosy?"

"Hook Cano's bunch. One of his men, Reboza, tried to rape me, the night Captain Caldwell died. This young Ranger named Travers happened along, pulled the man off me, and shot him dead when the Mex tried to throw a knife. I took Travers home, he's a handsome devil anyway, and I felt I owed him something. You know how it is, Lil?" Her tearful dark eyes were pleading.

"Sure, honey, I know how it is," Lily said, with dryness. "You showed good taste—in this instance, at least. I know Milt Travers. He's a fine boy, and almost too damn good-looking. But I thought Hook was going to protect you, even after he dropped you."

"That's what he promised." Rosita swallowed hard. "But it's all off now. He's afraid of what I might tell Trav. Everywhere I go, one of the bastards is there, eyeing me, nodding and grinning at me like a hyena."

"What could you tell Trav?"

"Nothing that I know of. Not a damn thing."

"Who did Hook drop you for?"

"I never knew."

"You know—but you don't dare tell," accused Lily.

"I don't know, Lil, honest to God." Rosita began to weep, vivid face in her tense hands, dark head drooping.

"All right, all right, baby," soothed Lily. "I'll give you the money."

"I want a loan. Not a gift. I'll pay it back," Rosita sobbed.

"You don't have to. Forget about it. What's fifty bucks between old friends? Are you sure that's enough?"

"That's plenty, Lil. Thank you, oh thank you so much!" Rosita brightened quickly. "You're saving my life. Prob'ly ain't worth much—to anybody but me. But thanks and God bless you, Lil."

"It's nothing, kid. I owe you anyway. You took care of me once when I was sick enough to die. I haven't forgotten that, Rosy."

"You're a good woman, Lil," declared Rosita, wiping her eyes with a lacy handkerchief. "Thanks again—and I'll see you sometime."

Lily Lavoy smiled. "You want me to tell Travers where you've gone?"

"No, no, I don't mean a thing to him. And he'd just get himself killed, if he came down there." Rosita shook her dark shimmery head.

Lily poured two crystal glasses full of claret, and they clicked rims and sipped. "Just where *will* you be, sweetie? I might want to get in touch with you, or let you know when it's safe to come back. The Rangers'll clean up this rotten town—in time."

"Chappy Chiapas's cantina in Galeana," said Rosita. "He's my uncle, my mother's brother, a good honest man."

"Thank God there are a few of 'em around." Lily noted the name and address on a white pad. "Any message for Milt Travers?"

Rosita smiled, almost shyly. "You can tell him I'll always remember that night."

"I wager he will, too." They finished their wine, embraced, and Lily let her out the back way, down the open stairway.

Back in the living room, Lily heard a knock on the front door. It must be Red Bush, she thought, with a smile of pleasure. Hasn't seen me around for a couple of days, getting worried—and maybe hungry. I hope, anyhow.

She was still smiling when she opened the door, but it froze on her lips, her whole body freezing with it. Standing there was a hulking heavy-shouldered man in greasy buckskin, his cruel coppery features impassive as granite, his eyes slits of black venom. *Quadah, the Apache.* Lily Lavoy knew she was dead in that instant.

She tried to slam the door shut, but the massive Indian pushed through it with ease and kicked it closed behind him. Lily Lavoy started to scream, as a great grimy hand clutched her white throat and lifted her into the air. Carrying her by the neck like a ragdoll, the Indian moved into the luxurious parlor, booted the door shut at his back, and flung her down on the carpeted floor hard enough to break her back and skull, driving all the breath from her lungs.

Lily Lavoy prayed for unconsciousness, but it did not come for a long time. By then she was praying for death.

* * *

Rusty Bouchard took another stroll through the Franklin Hotel barroom. Lily Lavoy was still absent from her favorite alcove table. Bouchard knew how she valued privacy and enjoyed spending a certain amount of time alone, but it wasn't like her to stay home three days and nights in a row. He decided to visit her place, even though she'd requested that he come only on invitation.

The hell with that. She might be sick or drunk or back on drugs again. Lily had been morbidly unhappy since the death of Rube Caldwell.

There had been a report of prowlers in the neighborhood of the Caldwell house, and Fox Edley had ridden up there to investigate and see Susan and the kids. Milt Travers was prowling about on foot, watching events involving the big augurs around the town hall and the sheriff's office and county jail across the street. Lashtrow was still down in Mexico with Ashley and the Anvil cowboys, chasing the rustlers and their stolen herd. Rammel and Donna Ashley hadn't yet checked in from Pinon, New Mexico.

Lash and Ram are doing all the work, seeing all the action, Bouchard reflected in disgust. While the three of us hang around El Paso and don't accomplish a goddamn thing. Save for Trav blowing away that Mex rapist.

Crossing the plaza toward the corner of Curtice Street, Bouchard was a broad knotted stump of a man with russet hair and beard, his powerful body propelled easily on stalwart bowed legs. One gun was sheathed openly on his right thigh, the other tucked in his belt under the suitcoat, in position for a left-handed draw. Red Bush had been practicing with his left lately. He wanted to get as good as Lashtrow with the left hand, but he doubted he ever would.

Electing to use the rear entrance, Bouchard climbed

the creaking outside stairs to Lily's veranda. The kitchen door was unlocked and he went in, sensing something wrong the minute he stepped over the threshold. An eerie hush hung on the air, with a queer raw odor he couldn't define. The doors along the corridor were open, but the rooms were empty. "Lily! Are you home, Lil?" he called. There was no reply, no sound at all. Nearing the parlor he recognized the smell of blood, with an icy clutch in his throat and breast, a sinking flutter in his stomach.

At the archway he recoiled in horror. There was blood splashed and spattered everywhere in the rich room. The bloody thing that had been a beautiful woman lay sprawled on the Persian rug. "Jesus H. Christ," Bouchard murmured, tongue and mouth gone desert-dry. He fought the compulsion to turn and flee from the macabre scene, not wanting any closer view. He grabbed a bottle from the cabinet and gulped from the neck of it. Like water in his numbed stricken bulk. "Oh *no,* no, *no!*" he moaned in utter misery, fury rising like a flame of madness within him. "That sonofabitch Injun! That goddamn Apache! The second time!"

Bouchard knew at once who had done this. He'd seen it before, years ago up in the Nations, the ravaged body of a lovely woman, who'd been raped, murdered, and mutilated in the very same way. His common-law Osage wife, Singing Bird. Quadah didn't have to take the scalp to leave his mark. The only recognizable part left of Lily Lavoy was her golden hair, spread awry on the thick-piled carpet.

Bouchard's stomach convulsed. Gagging, retching, he ran for the washroom, barely making it in time, and vomited until he was empty as a spent cartridge. He wondered how much the Apache had stolen. Not that it mattered now. Time enough to ascertain that later.

Right now there was just one thing in the world to do. *Kill Quadah.* Shoot the red bastard to ribbons. Make him die slow. Nothing would balance the scales, but at least that evil stinking sonofabitch would be dead.

Leaving the way he had entered, Bouchard thumped down the outside staircase and plunged through an alley toward the street. Slow down, cool off, take it calm and easy, he commanded himself. Go in the hotel saloon and belt down a few drinks. They don't serve Injuns. You gotta wait till the red haze clears from your brain, and your blood stops running like lava. You gotta regain full control, steady down, let your heartbeat and breathing slow to normal. You're an old-timer, not a goddamn kill-crazed kid. Easy does it, Red Bush. Cool and quiet, smooth and easy. You know the way. You oughta by this time, for chrisake. You been at it long enough. You was town marshal of Ellsworth, Kansas, long before you got to be a Ranger.

Bouchard went from the side street through the stained-glass door into the hotel saloon, the nearest and best bar, and was shocked to an abrupt halt. There was Quadah arguing with the white-coated bartender. It was coming sooner than anticipated, and Bouchard was glad of it. The Injun must have wanted a quick showdown too, or he wouldn't have come in here. He knew the Rangers stayed at the Franklin.

"I'm sorry but we don't serve Indians here. It's against the law," the bartender said. He was obviously repeating himself, patience wearing thin.

"No Injun," Quadah said. "Me Creole-Cajun. Want whisky."

"You look Indian to me. I'm sorry, mister."

"You be goddamn sorry, you don't serve. You be dead, white eyes."

Brown gaze sweeping the smoke-fouled room for

Mexicans, Bouchard walked up behind the big Apache. "You're under arrest, Injun."

Quadah turned with slow impassive dignity. "For what? For talkin?"

"For murder." Men were leaving the bar, getting out of the line of fire.

"You crazy, Red Beard." The obsidian eyes looked him up and down. "Who me kill, huh?" The bold predatory features were like reddish rock, the wide mouth downturned under the jutting nose, the jaws square and stolid.

"You murdered a white woman," Bouchard stated evenly.

"Huh?" It was a grunt of disgust. "You no draw gun." Quadah's slitted black eyes were fixed on the Ranger's right hand and holstered Colt. He himself wore two pistols openly on a double-sheathed belt.

"I don't need it till you make a move." Bouchard watched the Injun eyes.

"Who me kill, crazy man?"

"You killed Lily Lavoy." A long-drawn sighing sound stirred the blue smoke.

"You damnfool, wanta die?" Keeping his stare on Bouchard's still right hand, the Apache gestured in contempt and reached right-handed.

Red Bush knew from the Injun eyes that the move was coming, and he drew with his left hand and shot Quadah through the right arm, the impact jerking the Indian into a half-turn, his weapon clattering to the floor. Bouchard swerved his barrel to line on the buckskin-clad left arm.

Quadah reached left-handed then, and Rusty Bouchard drilled his left elbow, the bright blast like an echo of the first. The Apache retained the gun in his left hand, but the shattered arm could not lift it. The .45 blared through a brass cuspidor into the floorboards.

"You come with me now?" Bouchard asked, in level tones.

Quadah shook his long-haired black head, stoical as ever, and Bouchard's .44 blazed again, the bullet striking the broad chest and smashing the Apache back on the bar. He hung there helpless, bleeding from three wounds, his muscular broken arms dangling useless. The dirty bleached buckskins were splotched with scarlet.

"You gotta die hard and slow, Injun," said Bouchard. "Because of what you did to two women I loved."

Quadah swayed ponderously to and fro, only the bar holding him upright, but nothing showed in his cruel copper face. No pain, no fear, no regret—no emotion whatever.

"You know what you did to those women," Bouchard said, teeth on edge shining white through his red beard. "You know why I'm doin' this to you."

Quadah tried vainly to spit at him, a crimson drool streaking his chin. Bouchard slammed a slug into the abdomen, low down, and Quadah bounced off the mahogany to pitch forward on his face and writhe feebly on the floor. Sickening of the whole business, Bouchard hammered a shot through the Apache's skull and turned away, the smoking gun hanging loosely from his left hand. He felt nothing but nausea in his stomach, and the bitter taste of cordite in his mouth. The gunblasts reverberated in the room.

Rusty Bouchard just wanted to get away from everyone and everything. There was a bottle or two in his room, and he'd go up there to do his drinking. He walked wearily to the runway that led to the lobby, every eye in the saloon following him. Once he was gone, the babbling voices erupted in a frenzy from pent-up excitement, everybody talking at the same time.

ROE RICHMOND

Red Bush couldn't care less that he had carved another legend into the annals of the Texas Rangers, or that if this kept up he might become as famous as Lashtrow and Travers. He didn't know he already was, for that matter. He only knew he was tired, empty, and spent. He couldn't go back to Lily's. Someone else would have to clear up that horrible mess, and this one here, too. Rusty was done, finished for the day.

All Bouchard cared about at the moment was reaching the lonely security of his room upstairs, locking the door, and settling down to smoke his pipe and drink himself into the peaceful oblivion of sleep.

It would require a helluva lot of whisky, he knew full well.

THIRTEEN

The weather cleared and warmed after the storm, and the snow began melting. Lashtrow thought with dread of northern climes where a blizzard like that would strike and bury the land in white, and the snow would remain all winter, piled ever deeper by following storms. Down here the snow came and went, the grip of winter was not ironhard for months on end.

Halfway to Galeana they had once more picked up the wide churned trace of the cattle, still moving west toward the Sierra Madre. The rustlers must have got the stock into shelter in time to save most of the herd. They saw a few carcasses, near skeletons after the Mexes butchered them for meat, and the wolves and buzzards devoured the rest. But not many. Ashley's spirits were on the rise again, and Lash was relieved and hopeful.

Now the adobe pueblo of Galeana was in sight, spread erratically along the shores of the River of Sainte Maria. The cattle tracks detoured north to bypass the village and make a crossing, which must have been rough with the stream swollen by the runoff from melted snow. The sun had set early beyond the mountains, turning the western sky into a brief flaming forest fire. The lights of the settlement began to twinkle through the quick-closing blue and purple dusk. It was growing a bit colder as night came.

Mounts and men were bone-tired and gaunt, as Lashtrow led them into town and the cantina of Chappy Chiapas. Leaving their broncs at the hitchrail, they walked stiff-legged and numb-butted into the lights and warmth of the saloon, after Val Verde had checked the place out for members of the Cano crew. Their faces were raw-red and chapped from winter exposure.

Chappy himself, plump, jolly, and mustached, presided behind the bar. There were few customers, but a slim pretty girl was playing the mandolin on a tiny stage at one end of the room, a white flower in her black hair. Arizona's merry roving glance found her immediately, and he said, "For chrisake, Val, I know her." Val Verde looked her over with a critical squint. "She ain't bad," he admitted, without enthusiasm. Arizona laughed and said: "You're right, prune-face. She ain't bad. She's goddamn beautiful."

Chappy's deep-set eyes and full-moon face shone as he recognized Lash. "Order up, amigos. On the house for friends of Lashtrow." He extended a heavy gnarled hand and Lash grasped it. "How are you, Chap?" He introduced Ashley and the cowboys. Chiapas wasn't too interested in the other gringos, but his delight was plain at seeing Lashtrow.

"A long time, Lash," he said. "You look well and young as ever."

"Too long, Chappy. You don't grow old at all, man."

The four riders tossed off their free drinks, bought two bottles, and adjourned with their glasses to a table. Arizona was frowning as he sought to recall the mandolin player's name. Val Verde didn't look at her again. Mullen and Cobb sighed in satisfaction as they drank their whisky, knowing it was the best in the place, on account of Lashtrow.

At the bar Lash inquired, "A trail herd pass by lately?"

"Yesterday, Lash."

"Those cattle belong to Mr. Ashley here, Chappy."

"Figgered they was stolen when I heard who was drivin 'em. Hook Cano's men. It ain't the first rustled herd they've put by here."

"Any of the big ones, Chap?"

Chiapas shook his frosted graying head. "Just *vaqueros,* I believe."

"Yeah, the big boys turned back to Juarez. Where can we find the stock?"

Chiapas smiled and fingered his mustache. "I know where they usually hold 'em until the buyers come. A dead-end canyon about ten miles west. I'll show you on the map, Lash." He pulled a crumpled map from under the counter and smoothed it out on the wood.

The name had finally come to Arizona. *Rosita Shaw.* He spoke it aloud, stood up from the table, and ambled with leisurely grace to the stage. The girl ceased playing, surprise and vague hostility on her cameo-clear features. But Arizona had a casual, easy, and nonchalant manner, along with a frank boyish smile of admiration, which charmed most women instantly. He could swagger and look shy at the same time.

"Rosita Shaw, what are you doin down here on foreign soil?" he drawled amiably. "Don't you remember me? *The Conquistador* in Juarez?"

Her face lit up. "Oh, yes, I remember now. They call you Arizona. It was the only name I could get out of you. That was quite a party."

"It sure was. I never forgot dancin with you."

"Yes, it was fun." Her smile flashed back, as bright as his. "I just got here myself." She nodded at the bar. "My

123

uncle owns this place. I'm staying awhile with him."

"Chappy's an old friend of Lash's, huh?"

"Is that *Lashtrow?*" She stared at the tall Ranger, lounging on the counter to study a map with Chiapas and Ashley. There was an awed look, almost worshipful, in her great dark eyes. "I've heard so much about him. From my uncle and from Travers in El Paso. Trav's a Ranger, too."

"How were things in El Paso?" asked Arizona, slightly disconcerted by her interest in Lashtrow. When with him, most girls didn't pay any attention to other men. But in this case, Arizona couldn't blame her. Lashtrow was truly something, one in a million.

A shadow fell across Rosita's keen face and dulled her eyes with grief. "Not good, not good at all. You knew Captain Rube Caldwell was dead? Just before I left Lily Lavoy was murdered by an Apache named Quadah, who worked for Hook Cano."

"For godsake," Arizona said. "I didn't know Lily, but I heard about her, a course. Saw her once in the Franklin Hotel barroom, lookin like a queen with golden hair, a real beauty. That is a goddamn shame."

"She was a good friend of mine," Rosita Shaw said, in a shaky voice. "Lily lent me the money to come down here, the very day it happened." She shuddered violently. "Right after I left her house."

"Did they get the Injun?"

"Ranger Red Bouchard got him, but good. Shot him all to pieces in the Franklin saloon."

Arizona patted her shoulder. "You need a drink, Rosita," he said gently. "Come on over to our table and meet the guys I ride with. Nice fellas. The little one acts kinda sour, but it don't mean nothin. He's my best friend. What's your pleasure, little lady?"

"Sherry, I guess." She wanted claret but, thinking of

Lily, she couldn't pronounce the word without breaking into tears.

Arizona placed a chair for her, made the introductions, and went to the bar for her drink, and to tell Lash about the recent events in El Paso. Cobb and Mullen made the girl feel at home. Val Verde ignored her, but it was from shyness more than anything else.

Lashtrow listened gravely, his strong-boned features solemn, the gray eyes sorrowful. "Jeezus," he said softly. "That same goddamn Quadah killed Bouchard's Indian wife up in the Nations years ago."

"No wonder Red Bush blew the bastard all apart," Arizona said, and carried the glass of sherry back to the table.

Rosita had just finished telling the cowboys about the murder and swift reprisal in El Paso, and their stubbled faces were set like stone. She accepted the sherry and sipped gladly, needing something stronger.

"That whole Cano crew's gotta go," Cobb said grimly. "Every last one a them."

"They're goin, Cobber, for goddamn sure," Val Verde gritted.

"Let's drink to that." Arizona raised his glass. "We'll leave eight of 'em dead when we run off that herd tonight, boys."

"There'll be moon enough," said the ruddy-faced Mullen. "And the sky's good and clear."

Rosita Shaw gazed around at the four bleak wind-burned faces. "You're after the herd that passed by yesterday?"

"It belongs to Mr. Ashley, up at the bar with Lash. Anvil brand from New Mexico. They burned our spread down and rustled our stock. Us boys ride for Ash." It was a long speech for the hulking round-faced Cobb.

"This talk ain't for a nice young gal like Rosita," demurred Arizona. He smiled at her. "Wanta take a walk? My legs need stretchin. You'll excuse us, gents?"

"It was nice meeting all of you," Rosita said, rising with Arizona. "Best of luck to you."

A strikingly handsome couple, they walked out through the full-length wintertime door. Chiapas observed their departure with an inscrutable look.

Mullen wagged his early-balding head, a grin dimpling his red cheeks. "That Arizona's sure got a way with the women, smooth as satin."

"He's a natural-born whoremaster." Val Verde spat into a cuspidor. "All he thinks of is friggin."

"You don't like girls much, do you, Val?" said Cobb.

"Sure I like 'em," Val Verde swallowed three ounces of whisky. "But I'm scairt of the goddamn critters. Don't fear nothin else on the face a the earth, beast or bird or man. I'll fight anythin that walks or flies or crawls. But I'm scairt shitless a women. Don't make no sense, does it?"

"It's what makes you bitter as acid prob'ly, Val," said Mullen. "One good piece of ass, and you'd likely be damn near human."

"I ain't seen you guys gettin a helluva lot lately" Val Verde scoffed. "And even with Arizona, it's mostly just talkin about it."

"We'll fix that when we get back to El Paso," declared Cobb. "Git you fixed up too, Val. You ain't fit to live with the way you are, kid."

Lashtrow and the five Anvil men stood on the jagged rimrock overlooking the box canyon in which the herd was held. It was a clear cold night of overwhelming beauty, the moon not far past the full, the stars glittering with diamond brilliance. The wind had died with daylight, and the air was calm and still. The canyon branched off the plain to run north-and-south, at right angles to the course of the drive. There seemed to be more cattle than ever; the rustlers must have raided *rancherias* along the way. Ashley and Lash estimated there were 1500 head now.

Back in Galeana they had dined well at the cantina on enchilados, frijoles, burritos, and rice. Chappy arranged for them to swap horses at the livery, leaving their own to rest in the barn, switching saddle and gear to fresh mounts. They had checked their weapons and ammunition, spilling extra cartridges into jacket pockets. They were ready to steal back the Anvil stock, primed to kill the Mexicans to the last man.

There were eight *vaqueros,* as they had figured. Chacon was the only one Lash could identify at a distance, and he was evidently in command. They had set up camp in a walnut grove beside a small creek at the mouth of the canyon. They'd been using the Anvil horses for a *remuda*. Some of the broncs were recognizable to Ashley and his riders. They were picketed in a rope corral near the campsite. The Mexes had tents for shelter.

Trying to formulate a plan of attack, Lashtrow scanned the sweeping immensity of the heavens, picking out a few constellations he knew. The Big Dipper was outlined clearly, and the spaced stars of Orion's Belt. Arcturus flared in the west, high above the Sierra Madre, and Antares hung lower, a ruby in the southwest. To the southeast, Saturn was a steady saffron glow.

Far below two Mexicans jogged into the canyon to nighthawk the herd, while the other six settled down around the orange glare of the campfire, blanket-swathed against the chill night air.

It would be easy to wait until they were asleep in their

tents, and then wipe them out. But even against these Mexican killers, Lash hated to strike without warning. It was like murder, and he couldn't stomach it. Foolish in a matter like this, of course, but Lash couldn't help it.

The closed north end of the canyon, much less steep than the sheer sides, was accessible. They could drop down that slope, and start the herd moving toward the open end, stampede them through the enemy camp. Three men to push the cattle; three men outside the canyon mouth to turn the herd back eastward. That should work out all right.

The others listened intently to Lashtrow's plan of action.

Val Verde shook his narrow head. "Why not just hit the camp, all of us, and cut them six sonsabitches down? Take the other two greasers when we go in after the stock. That way, none a the bastards git away."

"You're a bloodthirsty little brute." Arizona laughed lightly. "But it's more fun to give 'em a fightin chance, take 'em on the wing."

"That's correct, Arizona," agreed Mullen. "I ain't got much heart for killen 'em in their blankets."

Cobb shrugged and spat tobacco juice. "Any old way's okay by me, boys. Just so I remember to grab me a Saltillo blanket on the way out."

"Always wanted a Saltillo myself," Mullen said.

Val Verde snorted. "Be nice if you can git the Mexican stink outa them."

"We'll do it Lash's way," decided Ashley. "How do we split up?"

Lashtrow considered briefly. "Ash, you take Cobb and Val out front to cover the mouth. Don't hit 'em, just wait for the herd and turn it east. I'll take Arizona and Mullen around back and get the ball rolling."

"All right, boys, that's it." Ashley led Cobb and Val

Verde to their horses, and they drifted downgrade toward the prairie floor, dewy white under the moon.

Lash and his pair of cowhands mounted and rode north along the stony summit toward the dead-end of the basin.

Arizona chuckled. "That little Val wanted to go straight in and eat 'em alive, didn't he?"

"That'd prob'ly be the safest and surest way," Lashtrow said, thoughtfully.

"That'd be raw murder," Mullen said. "I can't kill like that, no more'n you boys can." He looked down at the massed cattle on the canyon floor. "Them steers must be down to skin and bone."

"The grass down there looks pretty good," Lash said. "They've had a night and day of good grazing. That'll help some, Mul."

Mullen nodded. "Fifteen hundred head of prime beef'll bring about forty thousand dollars at the current rates. That's a neat bundle of *dinero* on the frontier, in this day and age."

"At least Ash can pay our back wages without breakin himself," Arizona said.

"You'll blow all a yours in a week, Arizona," said Mullen.

"Maybe so. Then I can start borrowin from you guys."

"Not me, by jeezus! I'm hangin onto every nickel this time, kid."

Arizona laughed at him. "Hell, Mul, you're the easiest touch there is. You've loaned out more cash than I ever earned. Your heart's bigger'n your head, Mully."

"I'm changin, by gawd," Mullen declared. "Goin save my dough and git married. Gittin too goddamn old to punch cattle."

Lashtrow was thinking abstractly about $40,000. That

represented a lifetime of hard work for Ash, the difference between comfortable success and total failure. He must owe a lot of it, but he'd have enough left to set up a business—or a new spread. The Ashleys deserved it. Lash was glad for them.

Edging his dappled gray bronc toward the rim, Lashtrow stared down the steep broken rock wall, with tangles of thorny nopal and agrito sprouting unexpectedly from fissures. At the bottom were mesquite thickets, threads of chaparral, and tall branched pillars of pitahaya. Bright moonbeams glinted on horned heads and a rippling stream. A good holding ground with abundant grass and water. Nearing the north end now, his gaze raked the rear wall, seeking the easiest route of descent. There was no easy way. He hoped these borrowed horses were surefooted and unafraid. A skittish mount, a tumbling fall, could get all three of them killed here, if the nighthawks were alert. Lash had been unable to spot the two Mexes who had come in there to ride circle. He wished he was on his sorrel tonight.

Slowly, warily, they picked a path down the inner slope of the back wall, mostly turf and dirt instead of stone. With Lash in the lead, they switched back and forth through cardenche, scrub oak, and boulders. The rattle of pebbles and the crackling of winter-dry brush were covered by the sounds of the cattle, mooing, lowing, or bellowing, as they shifted about to graze. But the moon was like a great searchlight, etching the landscape in silver and black. Surely they'd be seen and shot out of the saddle by Mexican marksmen below. No such thing happened. The night-riders must be on the far side of the stock, guarding the open south end.

Lashtrow took the stinging whip of stiff branches, and warmed his right-hand gun in his palm, easing the iron in and out of the cold leather. Hooves sparked on rocks, skidded in leaf-mould, and saddle gear creaked complainingly. The horses' shied and reared, snorting and nickering, fighting the reins, but the riders held them in rigid control. And the bottom seemed rising to meet them. At last they were all the way down, sweating slightly despite the cold. Lash's mouth was dry and he bit off a chew.

Leveled off on the canyon floor, they prodded the nearest cows into motion, gently at first, then increasing the pressure, until they heard the profane Latin cries of the two bandits as they toiled to hold the stirring animals. Unleashing ropes or quirts, the Americans began to drive in earnest, and the cattle moved faster, faster, until they were running.

Lash fired into the air, Arizona and Mullen followed suit, and the herd surged forward with a roar and rumble that set the frosty earth to shuddering. Panic spread and the stampede was on.

The outlaw pair fled frantically in front of the thundering torrent of horned beef, while Lash and Mullen and Arizona raced their horses through the boiling dust at the rear. It had all the wild exultance of a cavalry charge, and Lashtrow laughed aloud as he heard his comrades yelling like blood-mad Indian braves on the warpath. The two Mexicans had been veering to the left, looking for a niche or cranny to shelter in, the last time Lash glimpsed them through the duststorm. He swerved to that side with Mullen in his wake. Arizona racked along straightaway to keep the cattle at top speed. The entire universe was rocking eerily.

The Mexes had found a break in the cliff and yanked their ponies into it, clear of that avalanche of horned heads and drumming hooves. From a rock cornice they peered back, still mounted, to see what or who had spooked the steers. Their pistols flashed fiery jets, as they sighted the onrushing riders. With lead snarling and searing close about them, Lashtrow and Mullen threw down and fired from a gallop.

Lash saw the shape he'd targeted on reel and topple from the saddle into a drift of shale, his pinto bolting away alongside the hurtling millrace of the herd. Mullen's man, horse and all, went down floundering and threshing in the tazcal bushes. Passing in full stride, Lash slammed another shot into the dark sprawled figure on the heap of shale, and went racing on down the canyon edge, a sheer stone wall at his left and the flood-tide of beef on his right.

A horse screamed behind him, and Lashtrow reined his bronc in and around in a tight rearing turn that called for all his strength. Mullens's *grullo* was foundering, apparently gutted by a knife stroke from the fallen Mex in the tazcal brush. Flung clear, Mullen was bouncing and rolling and flailing in the grass. The slate-colored mustang plunged into the dirt, kicking and trumpeting in anguish, and Lash saw the dragging entrails. Gunflames slashed after Mullen before he ceased tumbling and slid to a stop on the ground. His body shivered under the shock of bullets.

Lashtrow lined on the muzzle lights and the crouched form in the brush, letting go to empty his Colt, which jumped in his right fist like a live thing. The Mex went to his knees, lurched backward and down in the tazcal, as Lash's slugs ripped him. But too late for Mullen, he feared.

Swinging down from the saddle Lash knelt beside Mullen, turned him over and lifted him carefully in his arms. Mullen tried to grin, but death was already in his eyes and face. Moonlight revealed it all too clearly.

"Thought I—had the bastard—dead," Mullen panted painfully. "Played possum, Lash—up with a knife—in my hoss's belly. Goddamn luck. Tell Cobb—and the boys—" A spasm shook him, blood drowned his words, and Mullen was gone. His eyes gazed vacantly up at the stars.

Lashtrow lowered him gently to earth, and climbed wearily upright, sorrow and rage mixed in him. Another good man gone under. Mullen would never collect his back pay, or marry, or get a Saltillo blanket—except as a shroud. Mullen who wanted to play fair, wouldn't commit murder. Poor old Mullen. Old, hell! Probably in his forties. The world had ended for Mully. The *grullo* was dead too, so Lash wouldn't have to shoot him.

Lash climbed back into the leather, after reloading his .44, the bronc rearing and circling in a frenzy of terror. Lash reined him down and spurred him into a gallop beside the thundering herd, pulling his rifle from its scabbard. There were six more Mexes up ahead.

At the canyon mouth, roused by the earth-shaking stampede, the bandits came stumbling and tripping out of their tents, carbines in hand, and fled for their saddled horses, intent only on escape from the rampaging cattle. They were mounted when Ashley and Val Verde and Cobb opened up with Winchesters and scythed down men and ponies. The outlaws attempted to fight back from the bare walnut trees, but Arizona and Lashtrow rode up to catch them in a scourging crossfire. The agonized screeching of outlaws and horses rose through the relentless pounding of the herd and the crash of gunfire. *Bandidos* and mounts went down in weltering dust and gunsmoke streaked with flame, as the Mexicans were routed into flight.

A lone mounted man and two riderless broncs ran the blazing gauntlet and escaped somehow into the outer shadows. All the rest died there under the merciless rifle blasts. Lash feared it was Chacon, the leader, who had got away. But the main issue now was to check and turn the herd.

The lead steers had slowed when the gunfire broke out in front of them, and the stampede lost enough momentum so that it wasn't too difficult to turn the herd eastward in the direction of Galeana. Once that was done, the riders let the stock go and regrouped themselves.

"Where the hell's Mully?" asked Cobb, counting faces and finding Mullen's missing.

"They got him back there in the canyon." Lashtrow went on to describe how it occurred, the Anvil men listening in grief-stricken silence. When Lash finished, the cursing began.

Cobb caught up a Mex pony with a saddle on it, and Arizona threw the finest Saltillo blanket he could find in the wrecked camp to him. Lash led them back to the bodies of the *grullo* and its rider. Very carefully they wrapped Mullen in the blanket and tied him across the saddle on the Mexican paint horse. They would give him a decent burial in Galeana.

The stampede had run itself out, the cattle milling about aimlessly or scattering across the open plain. They set about gathering the herd in the moonlit night, and pointing it back toward the Rio de Ste. Maria, Galeana, and Texas. Texas felt a thousand miles away.

Ashley and Lashtrow took the point, Arizona and Cobb the swing positions, and Val Verde brought up the drag and *remuda*. No one felt like talking; it was just as well they were widely separated in the moonlight.

FOURTEEN

"What the hell's goin on here, for chrisake?" Hook Cano, his darkly handsome visage contorted, glared around at his confederates, gathered in his secret living quarters above *El Conquistador Cantina* in Juarez. "We goin to let a handful of half-assed Rangers come in here and destroy our whole goddamn outfit? They got a good start already. They killed two of our boys in the Sacramentos. Rammel burnt down three more up in Pinon—Keech and Vargas and Stokes."

"Who the hell is Keech?" the squat Pablito asked, a twisted stogie in his protruding teeth. He was using a whetstone on the blade of his knife.

"He *was* our banker, one of our bankers." Cano's laugh was bitter. "We ain't got too many a that kind left." He hammered his steel hook on the flat, dented desktop. "In El Paso, Travers blasted our top rape artist, Reboza, and Bouchard shot the livin shit outa the Injun Quadah. Now I get this telegram from Chacon. He lost his whole crew down in Mexico, and Lashtrow and Ashley got their goddamn herd back. Ain't that somethin? Chacon ain't comin back, so we can count him dead."

135

"We could go down and take the cattle again," Tatum said, his tall frame at ease in a rawhide chair as he spun the cylinder of an ivory-handled Colt and puffed complacently on a thin cheroot.

Cano gestured with the hook. "I'm sick and tired of friggin round with that herd. We just lost *eight* men down there, for chrisake. Huffnail and Millhauser are standin by here, ready to buy the stock off Ashley, I understand. Let 'em have the herd. What we gotta do is smoke some Rangers, or we're done for. The big wheels in El Paso are disgusted with us. They'll really shit when they hear about the Anvil herd. I ain't tellin 'em, and you hombres ain't talkin neither. Let the news come by itself."

The ferret-faced Fasaro, dressed as usual in gaudy ornamented charro clothes, poured himself another mescal and savored the poisonous-tasting beverage. "Shouldn't be too hard to take care a three or four Rangers. We done it before."

"There's five of 'em," Cano said, lighting a brown cigarillo. "Rammel will be gettin here soon."

Tatum blew smoke rings. "These are a different brand of Rangers than we handled before. These are great gunfighters, every one of 'em."

"Balls!" said Cano. "I could take any one of 'em head-on, but it ain't practical. I can't advertise I'm a Ranger killer. I'm goin to be a big man in El Paso someday. If you horses' asses can't beat 'em, you can backshoot the bastards. You oughta be able to do *that* right, for the luvva christ! Trouble is you've grown soft, livin high and easy. Too much *dinero,* too much booze, too many whores."

Tatum grinned at him. "It hasn't toughened you up any either, Hook."

Cano eyed him with cold menace. "Don't get on the prod with me, man. You *know* I can take you, Tate."

"I keep hearin you can take anybody," Tatum laughed lightly. "But I don't see any signs of it."

"You wanta try me, Tate?" Cano started rising behind the desk.

Tatum and Fasaro both waved him down. "No time to be fightin amongst ourselves. *Madre de Dios,* what fools men are! It's time to stop talkin and start shootin. Words never won a war." Fasaro spoke in the same superior way he acted.

"Spare me your philosophy," Hook Cano said, with hauteur.

Pablito got up and tramped the floor with jingling spurs, wide and hunched with mad eyes, flared nostrils, and a beaver-toothed snarl. "This bunch's been goin to hell ever since you fell in love, Hook."

"We won't discuss that, amigo," Cano said, in icy tones. "And we better break up this meetin. I got a helluva lot to think about, *compadres.*"

"We all have, Hook," said Tatum, in a friendlier manner. "No hard feelins, huh?"

"Hell no!" Cano left his desk chair with lithe catlike ease, and poured drinks all around. "We gotta hang together, Tate."

"I got a notion that's just what we're goin to do." Tatum laughed ironically at his own gallows humor.

"You said Stokes was dead, Hook," Fasaro tasted his drink. "I heard he just got gunwhipped." He admired himself in the wall mirror.

"He did, he ain't dead. But he might as well be. He's still in a coma up there in Pinon. He and Chacon are both dead, so far as we're concerned. Chacon's headin for Mexico City, he said in the telegram."

Pablito chortled, contempt in his bulbous black eyes. "Chacon was afraid to come back, after botchin up and losin the herd and his whole crew." He was speaking normally, without the faked Mex accent.

"Maybe he was," Cano conceded. "I'd about decided to kill him anyway. When a man frigs up that bad, he's gotta go."

Tatum shook his shapely head. "We can't afford to bust our own men." His light skin marked him apart from the dark complexions around him. He thought he was as good-looking as Cano, but nobody else concurred.

Hook Cano laughed. "I wouldn't a killed him. But I sure was burned when I got his message." His partners were making ready to depart, and Hook added, "We'll meet here again tomorrow. Dinner up here at noon."

"It's that sonofabitch Lashtrow," grated Pablito. "He's gotta die, and I'm goin to see to that myself."

Cano shrugged. "One's as bad as another, Pab. They all got to go down."

After they left, Hook Cano paced the floor, a scowl on his handsome features, spurs clinking. He owned *El Conquistador,* but only his most intimate friends knew it. They weren't real *friends* either, he concluded.

He'd bought the cantina from the Chavez family, after its proprietor, the one-legged Chichi Chavez, had been shot to death in a gunfight with Ranger Rammel. It was Lashtrow who had blown off Chichi's leg, Cano recalled. Hook was never seen downstairs in the barroom or eating place, and he always came and went by a secluded rear door and narrow back alley. His presence in *El Conquistador* was a sound secret, lasting longer than he would have believed possible.

Hook Cano's brain was flitting about like a caged bird in his skull, darting crazily from one topic to another, giving him a headache. He paused to regard himself in the mirror. A good-looking, well-built man, with a widow's peak of wavy black hair, luminous brown eyes, and a winning smile. Right now the eyes weren't dancing and the lips were not smiling. Hook wasn't as vain as the rat-faced Fasaro, but he had more right to be. Tatum wasn't bad to look at, but he lacked Hook's charm, grace, and personality. Women had been easy for Hook Cano, ever since he could remember. Except for Amanda Ashley. He winced at that memory.

But the one he had now was not easy. She was tearing him apart inside, driving him to the verge of madness. Hook was getting paid back for all the girls he had hurt, left ruined and heartbroken. This woman would kill him, or get him killed, if he didn't get rid of her first. But he loved her, couldn't face living without her. For once in his life, Hook Cano wanted and needed a woman more than she did him. He didn't like that a goddamn bit, but there was no escaping it.

He splashed out another tall drink of Spanish brandy, sipping it as he walked around.

We had it made, everything smooth and sweet as syrup, until Lashtrow and those other Rangers came into the picture. Pablito was right—Lashtrow must die. Likewise Rammel, Bouchard, Travers, and Fox Edley. All five of the gringo sonsabitches.

Hook Cano had always believed he could beat any man in the world with a sixgun. He still did—almost. He wasn't so sure about Lashtrow.

That little bitch Rosita Shaw's left town too, they tell me. The thoughts went on ricocheting through Cano's mind. She was getting to be too much of a danger to me. That's why I sent Reboza to rape and strangle her. But he bungled it, got himself killed by Travers, and then Rosy took Travers home with her, into her bed, and God knows what she told him about me. I think she knows about this last woman, but I doubt if she's told anyone—yet. Too goddamn scared. But she knew I'd learn about her laying Travers, and wouldn't protect her anymore. After the Injun mangled Lily Lavoy, Rosita beat it across the border—or somewhere. She isn't in Juarez, so she must've gone farther south—or maybe up north.

She won't dare to come back, so I can forget about Rosita Shaw. She won't return to El Paso—*until I'm dead.* Hook Cano went cold all over and shivered deep inside, as that thought flickered into his head.

Well, nobody lives forever, everyone dies when his time comes. Even Hook Cano. So what the hell's the sense of worrying? He tried to regain his old devil-may-care attitude, but couldn't quite make it. Hook Cano wanted to live forever.

And it was then, perhaps for the first time, that Hook realized a chilling fact: The world would go on the same as ever, after his death, scarcely noticing he was gone. One man's death was like a leaf falling.

Cristo! But I am getting to be morbid. I gotta cut loose from that kind of thinking. A man invites death when he starts thinking about it all the time. You should laugh it off and act like you're going to live eternally, even though you know it's a goddamn lie.

Hook Cano refilled his glass with Fundador, took a long draft, and his spirit began to rise and soar on the wings of false bravado.

Go with your head high, a sparkle in your eyes, and a smile on your face, he instructed himself with a gay laugh. To hell with taking it too serious. Frig 'em, one and all.

That was the brandy talking, not Hook Cano. The awareness of this made him feel like a man mired and sinking in quicksand. A horrible helpless sensation. The harder he struggled the deeper he sank. He longed for the total escape into nothingness that morphine had brought him in the hospital, after they operated on his right hand. The soft feathery floating away into perfect peace, comfort, and contentment.

His glass was empty again, he noticed with surprise. Cano raised the bottle and drank straight from it.

The next day there was a conclave in the mayor's office in city hall. Amos Essling sat plumped in his black-cushioned chair behind the huge paper-strewn desk, pulling irritably at his veined nose, hooded eyes nearly shut. Judge Milo Bascomb, impeccable in tailored tweeds, smoked a slender cheroot and lolled fully relaxed at the mayor's right, while Sheriff Kriewold stretched his scarecrow length on the left, his lipless mouth slashed down like a scimitar to his thrusting chin.

They were waiting, without much patience, for Leo Fribance and Yeager.

"Bastards are always late," said Kriewold, loosing a brown stream of tobacco at a spittoon. "Yeager's prob'ly shovelin shit and Leo's countin his goddamn money."

Essling forced a short laugh, and Bascomb eyed the sheriff with distaste. Sometimes his seedy associates made the tall young judge want to throw up, and he might just do that today when Yeager came in stinking of the stockyards. Bascomb doubted if Yeager had bathed all winter, or even changed his reeking clothes. Hook Cano's crew were more desirable companions than these political parasites.

"Things ain't goin good nohow," Kriewold complained, spitting again.

Bascomb smiled coldly. "That's putting it mildly. Perhaps you should put your army of deputies to work for once. Must be *something* they can do, somewhere."

"I don't need no advice from a young shyster asshole

141

like you," Kriewold said, straightening in his chair and hitching at his gunbelt.

"You need it from someone," Bascomb said placidly. "Your department is becoming the laughingstock of the county. You'll never be reelected, not even as dogcatcher."

"Git off me, boy, or I'll blow your brains out!" rasped Kriewold.

Bascomb laughed.

Leo Fribance made his entrance then to interrupt the argument, overcoat on his arm, silk hat on oily head, freshly barbered and redolent of Bay Rum. He wore a costly plaid suit that fitted him poorly. Fribance smiled, nodded around, and took a chair in front of the desk.

"Greetings, gentlemen," the Copper King said, trying to sound like Bascomb. Only Essling replied with an unintelligible grunt.

Seconds later Yeager came storming in, squinted eyes and pocked face wild with anger. "They lost the goddamn Anvil herd down near Galeana, and seven of 'em got shot to death by Lashtrow and Ashley's cowhands. Only Chacon got outa it alive, and he's quittin. He ain't comin back."

"How do you know this, Yeag?" asked Bascomb coolly, as the other listeners sat rigid and silent.

"I just come from the Western Union. Saw a copy of the telegram Chacon sent Cano. The operator's my man, yuh know." Yeager wore a dirty old canvas jacket and smelled strongly of the stable. He sat down near the judge. Bascomb wrinkled his nose and moved his chair a few feet away.

"We better break with Hook," he said. "They can't do anything right lately. If the general populace finds out about our relationship, we'll all be out of office."

"Frig the general populace," Kriewold said. "We

need Hook and his boys. Gotta have guns, with them goddamn Rangers around."

"You have about twenty so-called gunmen wearing deputy's badges," pointed out Milo Bascomb. "Use them, Krie, for godsake. Let 'em earn their salaries for a change. They've been deadweight so far."

Essling nodded pompously, bald head gleaming. "You're right, Milo. Absolutely right."

Kriewold stood up, towering over the room, and settled his cartridge belt. "By the jeezus, I've stood all this shit I'm goin to!" His pale eyes were fixed on the immaculate Bascomb.

Bascomb rose and moved out to the center of the room, away from the rest. Kriewold stalked out and stood facing him, at about fifteen feet, panting with restrained fury.

"You want to draw on me, go ahead, Sheriff," said the judge tauntingly.

Kriewold laughed in derision. "You ain't even gotta gun, you fool!"

Bascomb unbuttoned his tweed coat, so they could see the pearl-gripped pistol in his belt. Everyone gaped in surprise, especially the sheriff.

Bascomb smiled. "Come on, Sheriff, go for it. You've been threatening to for weeks. Let's see that draw you boast about."

The other men sat silent and motionless. This was a new side of the debonair young judge, a complete transition, a different man altogether.

Kriewold stood on wide-planted boots, his thin chest rising and falling, the cords in his raw neck standing out in strain. "You ain't no gunhand, boy. I won't take advantage. Forget it, for chrisake!"

"Draw or get out!" Bascomb's voice was soft, quiet and deadly. "You're finished here."

143

Kriewold couldn't believe his own ears. He hung on the brink of drawing, but something in the judge's cold clear eyes stayed his hand. "Aw, frig it," he mumbled, turning away and walking doorward.

"You shyster sonofabitch!" Kriewold halted abruptly, pivoted in a full turn, but his large hands were empty, well clear of his guns. "Everything was okay until you— you—"

"Shut up!" Bascomb said sharply. "Shut up and get out."

"It all started when you—"

Quick as light, Bascomb pulled the pearl-handled .45 from his waistband and shot the sheriff in the belly. Kriewold gasped, doubled up, and lurched backward on jerking legs, pawing at his holster. Bascomb stitched slugs up his middle, breastbone and throat, the muzzle flames almost merging, the reports blending into one shattering blast.

Driven back on stomping high heels, his front crimsoned instantly, Kriewold's slumped shoulders struck the wall, his big-nosed face stupid with shock and disbelief. Groaning, he keeled slowly forward and crashed face-down on the floor like a tall chopped tree. Bright arterial blood spread beneath him. He never stirred again.

Bascomb whirled on the others, smoking gun poised. They were on their feet, Fribance and Yeager starting tentative draws, but their hands dropped, loose and empty, horrified expressions frozen on their features.

"For the luvva jeezus," whimpered Amos Essling. "What'd you do that for, Judge? You gone crazy, for chrisake?"

"Who'll miss him?" Bascomb said carelessly. "He was nothing as a sheriff and less than that as a man. He was no good, Amos."

144

Essling was in a dazed stupor. "What we goin to do for a sheriff?"

"Appoint one of the deputies." Bascomb smiled indolently. "Any one of them will do better than Kriewold. Drumm's the man for the job, I'd say."

"Christamighty!" said Yaeger. "You're a goddamn gunslinger, Milo! I didn't even know you *had* a gun."

"Most people don't," Bascomb said. "Better that way, I calculate." He thrust the weapon back under his belt.

"A real pro," muttered Fribance. "I never woulda believe it, Milo."

"On the frontier," Bascomb said smoothly, "a man has to be able to defend himself—or he's dead."

He was already walking toward the door when somebody pounded on it. Bascomb opened it narrowly so no one could see the interior, and smiled with composure at two anxious-eyed cops in uniform. "It's all right, boys, no trouble. Just trying out a new gun." The policemen grinned in relief and returned to their posts at the head of the staircase.

"What'll we do with the body?" Essling was quavering, as the judge came back to the desk.

"Bury it," Bascomb said dryly. "With great ceremony and all the honors due a sheriff who died in the line of duty."

"Who'll we say killed him?" demanded Fribance.

"Hook Cano's renegades. Or the Texas Rangers." Bascomb laughed airily.

"God above," moaned Essling. "This is a terrible thing, right in my own office! I don't know what made you do such a thing, Milo."

"Kriewold was getting to be a liability. We couldn't afford to have him around anymore. He talked too much and he lied too much." The others were still stupefied, gazing at the fresh-faced judge in awe and wonder, wagging their heads somberly. They avoided looking at the lank form on the floor.

Milo Bascomb smiled sweetly at them. "It'll be all right, boys, you'll see. Everything will be fine and dandy." His voice and manner were soothing and reassuring. He spoke as if addressing bewildered children, while pondering the best way to handle this matter.

Bascomb had planned this in advance. It was time to definitely establish, once and for all, that he was the head man.

FIFTEEN

The weather stayed fair and clear for the fifty-odd mile
ride from Pinon to Oregrande, for which Rammel was
thankful on account of his two female companions. It
was unseasonably warm, even up in the Sacramento
Mountains, so close to being balmy that it was like a
premature false spring. Donna Ashley and Melissa
Johnson were good equestrians and saddle-mates. Rammel had a slight sense of being encumbered and slowed
on the trail, but it was a pleasant burden withal.

Beautiful mountain vistas opened on all sides, rocky
knobs, cliff faces, barren or evergreen slopes, dashing
creeks and white-spumed waterfalls. The lower passes
were damp but clear of snow, and the sun shone with
unnatural brightness and warmth for midwinter. Rammel kept a vigilant lookout for hostile horsemen, who
might have been sent from El Paso to follow up on
Vargas and Stokes.

Back in Pinon, Vargas had been buried beside Keech,
red-flannel underwear and all, while Stokes still lay in a
coma from Monk Moncrief's gun-whipping, bedded
down at Dr. Ward Bailey's place. Rammel had been disappointed at being unable to interrogate Stokes, but he
had been present one day when the outlaw surfaced near

enough to semi-consciousness to mumble a few phrases:

"Wrong . . . everythin gone goddamn wrong . . . since the boss took up with—that woman." The voice croaked on but the rest was unintelligible.

Rammel decided that his first venture, in El Paso or Juarez, would be to discover the identity of Hook Cano's current object of love. Hook had a spectacular record as both lady- and man-killer.

In some of the highland passages, Rammel saw traces of the Anvil trail herd, still evident in spite of subsequent snowstorms. Pointing them out to the girls, he said, "They got through all right. With Lash along they couldn't miss."

"Oh, I hope so, I hope they're safe," Donna Ashley said, and then turned antagonistic, as she was wont at times. "This Lashtrow you're forever raving about. Is he God?"

Rammel grinned. "Damned close to it."

"Keech used to say only God could kill *him.*"

"In that case, one of the disciples did it."

"The ego and conceit of you Rangers!" Donna gestured in disgust.

Rammel laughed easily. "You're all wrong there, baby. By the way, how did you ever get involved with a man like Keech? You've never explained that, Donna."

"I don't have to!" She straightened in the saddle, then slumped. "I don't know anyway. He must have hypnotized me. Those eyes of his." She shivered. "I've never seen eyes like Keech's."

Melissa Johnson spoke. "That's true, he had hypnotic power. He used it on me, put me under a spell. Black magic or something. It was very powerful."

"Both you girls should've done better," Rammel stated. "Weren't there any men of your age available?"

"There was Arizona, who rode for us." Donna smiled reminiscently. "But he never had a serious thought in his head. My folks wouldn't have settled for a cowboy any-how. Especially for a gunhand."

"They preferred a *doctor*—like Keech?"

Donna glared at him.

"Arizona was very handsome," Melissa put in. "And a lot of fun."

"An empty-headed kid gunfighter," scoffed Donna Ashley.

"But a helluva lot better than the good doctor." Ram pressed the needle home with malice.

"Must you persist in talking about—*that?*" Donna demanded.

"I'm sorry."

Melissa attempted a more pleasant theme. "I'm glad old Doc Bailey got a second chance. There's a good man, and he's doing a fine job."

"You should've stayed with him," Donna declared.

"I may go back when I'm fully straightened out." Melissa knew the other girl resented her presence. Donna had wanted to be alone with Rammel on this long journey, although it would have done her no good. They'd both been despoiled by Keech, and the clean-faced Virginian wanted no part of them, Melissa realized. But Donna refused to admit this.

Rammel was musing that three was an awkward and difficult number. Without intention, it somehow always became two-against-one. When Ram talked to one of the women, the other felt left out. When the girls conversed, Ram had the feeling of an outsider. It was always that way with three people, even in one-child families. Which reminded Ram that he and Tess should have another kid soon. He didn't want little Trav growing up in the triangle that inevitably developed with three persons living together.

He and Travers had talked about this human phe-nomenon. Trav agreed and said it was something he intended to use in a book sometime.

Rammel considered his own position in this peculiar triangle. Out in the mountain wilderness with two pretty young women, both of whom were attracted to him. He could have had one or both, but he was resolved to take neither. Not simply because they'd been stained and sullied by Keech, but because he was determined to be faithful to Tess and his son. He told himself this, at any rate, with something less than absolute certainty. The mountain air had a fresh springlike softness, the girls were lovely and desirable—and Ram was still quite young, the quick hot fire of youth running strong in his blood. The hunger for feminine flesh that burned in any normal young man.

The second night out they made camp in a small nook beside a tiny creek, sheltered on one side by a rocky ledge, on the other by pines and spruces. Rammel gathered wood, kindled a fire, attended to the horses, and set up the tent, while the girls unpacked and prepared supper. After eating, and washing the utensils, they sat around the fire talking and drinking a bit of brandy from tin cups.

Melissa was strangely withdrawn and remote, not her usual cheerful self at all. She insisted she was okay, but her companions knew otherwise. She was near to suffering a remission. Swallowing some pills prescribed by Doc Bailey, saying she was just tired from the trail, she went to the tent early. Donna tried to snuggle closer to Rammel, but he gently rebuffed her.

"Go to hell!" Donna flared, and flounced off into the tent, leaving Rammel to drink alone and stare into the red-gold flames. He hoped the mulatto girl wasn't going to be ill. It was bad enough to travel with two healthy women, let alone a sick one. He didn't really *like* girls well enough to be constantly in their company. It was much better to ride with men.

That bastard Keech, thought Ram. There's one man I'm not sorry about killing. God only knew how many women he'd ruined in his abbreviated lifetime.

Waiting until sure the girls were sleeping soundly, Rammel crawled into his bedroll and hauled the tarp over it, having placed his gunbelt and Winchester close at hand. His head rested on the smooth-worn saddle. The night air was scented cleanly with the fragrance of woodsmoke, pines and spruce trees. A moon just past the full was shining high above, gilding the mountain domes and peaks. He thought about Trav and Lash, Red Bush and the Fox, and silently prayed they were all right, safe and unhurt. Caldwell, too.

He had no means of knowing, of course, that about this time, far away to the southwest in Old Mexico, Lashtrow and the Anvil men were standing on rimrock overlooking a box canyon, in which the stolen Ashley herd was grazing in the moonbeams. Strained with the tension that precedes combat.

Finally Ram faded into restless troubled sleep.

Eyes crusted, mouth parched, Rammel awoke in the middle of the night to the sounds of frightened horses neighing, whickering, snorting, and rearing frenziedly against their picket ropes. To his surprise he saw a lantern glow inside the tent, and heard some kind of commotion there.

Flinging off the tarp and kicking out of the blankets, Ram grasped his Winchester and came to his feet, glad he had left his boots on. He searched the fir trees for movement. Nothing. Then his blood froze as he saw some specie of big cat crouched on the stone shelf above the horses, luminous eyes on the broncs as if to choose one for a target. The huge sleek beast was about fifty yards from Ram, on a plane higher by ten yards or so.

A beautiful but menacing creature. Ram wondered if it were a cougar, mountain lion or panther; it was too big for a bobcat.

Rammel levered a cartridge into the firing chamber, and the great cat diverted his blazing yellowish orbs from the horses to the man, muscles rippling under the hide as it shifted to face Rammel and crouched ready to spring from the ledge. The predator seemed to recognize the threat of the rifle and man, losing interest in the horses at once.

Raising the Winchester to his right shoulder, Rammel took quick, careful aim and squeezed the trigger, the butt jarring hard against him, flame spurting on an upward slant, the report splintering the moonlit night. Ram was sure he'd scored, but the cougar launched itself into a tremendous leap toward the Ranger, apparently unscathed. Rammel fought the compulsion to turn and flee, knowing he was dead if he tried to run away. The huge cat would be all over him, ripping and slashing him to ribbons.

Working trigger and lever swiftly, standing firm and steady, Rammel got off two hipshots while the cougar was hurtling through the air straight at him, and he glimpsed spouts of dust from the tawny skin as the .44 –40s struck home. The cat landed in a broken sprawl, the dust smoking up, and Ram knew it should stay down as he jacked another shell into place. But it didn't stay down. Clawing to its feet as if untouched, the mighty creature came on, roaring and snarling, fast and graceful.

Bullets can't stop the goddamn thing, Rammel thought in panic, once more resisting the desperate urge to break and run. He fired twice more, the last slug tearing off the top of the lion's head, and the magnificent brute plunged to earth, rolling slackly, not more than ten feet from Ram's boots. There was blood from previous wounds on the gleaming hide, but it had taken the head-shot to bring the animal down. Some cat.

Rammel was breathless and sick to his stomach, scalp creeping, legs trembling, and spine a column of ice. "Jesus Christ," he murmured softly, in thanksgiving, and shook his head that shone silvery in the moonlight.

Donna Ashley burst out between the tent flaps. "God in heaven, what was *that?*" Then she saw the monstrous cat, and swayed on the brink of swooning.

"Panther, mountain lion, cougar, I don't know." Rammel reached out to hold the girl upright. "Never saw one before. Sure took a lot of killing. What's wrong in there?" He nodded at the tent.

"Melissa's having a bad spell. First she was burning up. Now she's freezing, shaking hard enough to break apart. I can't keep her warm, Ram. You'll have to help me."

"Sure, I'll do what I can." Rammel reloaded the rifle, laid it aside, and bent down to dig out the brandy bottle and two cups. "We both need a drink, baby. I'll have to get rid of this dead cat first."

After a couple of drinks, Rammel looped his rope around that bloody neck and dragged the carcass away from camp into the woods. "You were a tough one, old-timer," he said. "One helluva cat. Sorry—I had to—kill you." The body was incredibly heavy, and new warm sweat mingled with the cold on Rammel, as he tugged and panted.

Back by the campfire embers, he had another swig of brandy, and went to the picket line to calm and soothe the four horses, gratified that none of them had busted loose and run away.

"Come on, Ram, *come on!*" entreated Donna, from the canvas entry.

"I ought to stay outside, in case that cat has a mate around here," Rammel said, his gaze probing the ledge of rock, his Winchester back in hand.

"No, no, you've got to help me," Donna declared. "Between us we can warm her up."

Rammel sighed and followed her into the tent, where lanternlight flickered. Melissa was sleeping or unconscious, beads of perspiration glistening on her brown cheeks, her body shaking as if with convulsions.

"Take that side." Donna pointed. "Get in under the blankets, hold her in your arms. This is no time for Cavalier gentleman folderol, goddamn it! Get in there, Ram!"

Feeling ridiculous and embarrassed, Rammel crawled in under the blankets to embrace the mulatto girl, her ripe curved body vibrating against his. Donna got in on the other side, pressing as close as possible against Melissa's back. It grew warm and then hot, and the violent trembling gradually lessened. After a timeless interval of torture for Rammel, Melissa stopped shaking altogether and sank into peaceful slumber.

"There, she'll be all right now—I think," Donna whispered.

"I've got to get outa here," Rammel said, rolling out of the blankets, tucking them back in around the sleeping woman.

Before Rammel could rise, Donna was around the pallet and on top of him, utterly shameless in her passion. "No, you're staying with me, Ram," she panted. "You have to—put me to sleep—now. I'm afraid, I'm lonesome, I want and need you." She was clutching and clinging, her mouth searching for his, her body molded against his long lithe frame.

Fending her off the best he could, Rammel said: "Listen to me, girl. I've got to stand watch outside. Those big cats mate and travel in pairs, I understand. If that one had a mate, she could hit here any minute."

Donna went on straining and squirming against him,

hanging on with arms and legs, the feminine smell of her smothering him.

In final desperation, Ram grasped her upper arms roughly and threw her away from him. She lay there sobbing. Ram got up and stood over her, sweating and disheveled and miserable. Breathless and aching with desire.

"I'm sorry—Donna. I didn't mean—to hurt you. But we're all—in danger—here."

"Get out—you sonofabitch!" Donna Ashley sobbed. "Get the hell away—from me. And stay away!"

Rammel strode out from under the canvas, and filled his lungs with fresh pure mountain air. His green eyes scoured the perimeter of the campsite. No sign of another cougar yet. He sat down with his back against a rough boulder, bottle in his left hand, rifle at his right side. Settled for the long vigil until daybreak, Ram drank from the bottle.

"Women!" He made an epithet of it. "Goddamn women." Ram looked at the gray tent and spat in the same direction. Faint sounds of weeping still issued from the canvas.

It was colder and he rose to shrug into his corduroy winter jacket, taking a blanket back to the boulder. He resumed his seat, lifted the bottle, and stared again at the tent. "I'll take a mountain lion anytime." Rammel drawled.

In the morning Melissa was much better, weak and drowsy from medication but recovered enough to ride. Donna did not look at or speak to Rammel. They took it slow and easy on the trail, and still made Oregrande, a crude raw foothill settlement, before nightfall. The sidewalks were beaten clay paths.

There was no stagecoach for El Paso until tomorrow. It was just as well since Melissa required a good night's sleep and rest in a real bed. They obtained rooms in a nameless hotel. Melissa went immediately to bed, while Rammel stabled the horses in the livery barn.

The hotel served no meals, but the clerk recommended a café down the street. After washing up Rammel and Donna left the ramshackle hostelry and walked toward the eating place in silence. Until Ram indicated the short carbine in Donna Ashley's hand, and said, "Why are you carrying that around?"

"I feel safer with it."

"You don't regard me very highly as a protector?"

"I don't regard you as anything," Donna said frigidly. "Nothing at all."

It was still daylight. The lowering sun crimsoned windows across the street, and a dark form on a board awning blurred across reddened glass. Donna caught the movement, saw the rifle lined on Rammel.

"Get down Ram!" Donna cried suddenly, pushing him forward, swinging her carbine up and firing swiftly.

Rammel felt the hot suction of lead across his back, as he drew and hit the dirt on his chest. On top of the rifle blast came the bark of Donna's carbine, the flash of muzzle light. Rammel saw the sniper now, and scrambled about to bring his Colt to bear, but the man was already screaming and falling headfirst from the overhang into the street. A Mexican landing in an upheaval of dust, sprawling motionless.

Rammel was up, bronzed cheeks burning with shame as he crossed the street, unfired .44 in hand, Donna coming after him, her carbine cocked and ready. Doors slammed open and people rushed outside to head for the scene. Ram rolled the greaser over on his back. He was barely alive, a scarlet stain spreading from the center of his chest, his eyes dulling.

"Hook Cano sent you," Rammel said, more a statement than question.

Blood seeped from the man's lips, but no words came.

"Tell me one thing. Who is Hook Cano's girl?" Ram spoke hastily, urgently, his hands on the dying sniper's shoulders.

"How I know?" the Mex panted painfully. "Who the hell care? . . . I heard—it was—Caldwell's widow." The eyes went vacant as a spasm shook him, and he was gone.

Rammel turned to Donna Ashley. "Did you hear that? Rube Caldwell's dead and Hook Cano's courting his widow. Doesn't seem very likely, but who the hell knows?" He brushed red clay off his jacket and trousers.

"Yes, I heard." Donna had been covering Ram's back, her bright hazel eyes sweeping the ranks of on-lookers for other hostile Mexican faces.

A man said there was no law in town, but they had seen the Mex take the first shot; there wouldn't be any trouble. A clear case of self-defense. Rammel showed his Ranger badge to reassure the townspeople, and they went on toward the café. Donna said: "I don't seem to have any appetite."

"That was great shooting, Donna," said Rammel. "I'm the one who needs protection, I guess. You should try to eat something."

"I'm not very hungry now," Donna said. "I never shot anyone before."

"You saved my life, baby. If that means anything. Apparently it doesn't mean much to you."

"I'd have done it for anybody." There was a roguish look in her sparkling eyes and perky face. "But I'm kin-da glad it was you, Ram."

"Well, I'm sure glad you brought that carbine along." Rammel smiled down at her. "I owe you, Donna. I owe you a big one."

"There are ways of paying, Ram," she said, with a piquant grin.

SIXTEEN

Milt Travers and Fox Edley were working late in the second-floor Ranger office, trying to get caught up on the official reports, correspondence, and general paper-work that the secretary and office boy had neglected since Rube Caldwell's death. Travers was doing the bulk of it, with an effortless skill and speed that astounded the Fox.

"You're damn good at this kinda stuff, Trav," he said.

"I hate it." Travers went on writing. "Almost rather shovel out the stables. The Rangers are getting as bad as the Border Patrol."

Edley dropped his pen and leaned back in the swivel chair, forking out a plug of tobacco and gnawing off a chew. "Can't write no more. Hands gettin all cramped up." He looked fondly at Trav's dusky blondish head bent over the roll-top desk. "What d'yuh thinka Sheriff Kriewold's sudden departure?"

"Something funny there, Fox. Looks like an inside job to me. Judge Bascomb and Drumm, the new sheriff, had their heads together a lot before Krie caught it."

"A lot of funny business goin on. I keep seein Mexes hangin around Susan Caldwell's neighborhood. They don't do nothin, just fade outa sight. But what the hell they doin up there?" Edley made the spittoon ring with a brown stream. "Sometimes there's a closed carriage or a covered wagon."

"You think there's anything to that rumor we keep hearing about Sue and Hook Cano?" asked Travers, without missing a stroke of the pen.

"Hell, no! Susie's taken to drinkin kinda heavy, but she couldn't sink that low. She was a nice girl from a good family, a real lady."

"I didn't believe so either. But there's a lot of gossip about 'em."

"Yeah, there sure is." Edley shook his head gloomily. "Yuh know, Trav, I still don't believe Rube killed himself. Can't quite swaller that one."

"Where'd Red Bush go tonight, Foxcroft?"

"Prob'ly across the river prowlin around huntin for Hook Cano's hideout. He's apt to get himself killed over there, with that red hair and beard. Like a red flag to a bull, that's how it affects them greasers."

"Rusty took Lily Lavoy's death hard," murmured Travers, pausing to relight his cheroot.

Edley nodded. "He really went for Lil, and who'd blame him? She was a lotta woman."

"What do you think of that news from Pinon? Rammel wiping out three bandits up there."

"It reminds me I ain't done a damn thing here myself," said Edley, a scowl of self-disparagement on his lean tough features, the yellow eyes shadowed. "You got that raper, Reboza. Bouchard blew down Quadah, the one he wanted most. And God knows how many Lash has put under. I ain't hit anythin yet." The scarred leather face was mournful.

Travers laughed. "Your turn'll come, Fox. Plenty of them left." Travers resumed writing.

Edley admired the finely-cut profile and remembered his first meeting with Travers, way back in 1870 during buffalo season on the Staked Plains. Their liking had been instantaneous and mutual. Fox Edley had been riding outside the law then, but he switched to the right side after getting to know Trav and Lashtrow. They were only kids then, about twenty years old, he reflected incredulously, and I was only twenty-five myself. We've been together ever since, well over a decade. You could say my life started when I met those two boys. A whole new and better life.

"You decided anythin about Priscilla yet, Trav?" he inquired, shyly.

"Not really. Can't seem to make up my mind, Fox." Travers' smile was inscrutable, a faraway look in his clear blue eyes.

"Well, I'd sure hate to see you go, Trav, but it'd be the smart thing to do, I reckon," said Fox Edley.

"The hard part would be leaving you guys," Travers said gravely. "If it weren't for that, I'd resign in a minute. I want to marry Priscilla Cabot and I want to write books. I think it's what I was meant to do, Fox. But I don't want to leave you and Lash and Ram and Red Bush. That's the hell of it." He stared at a dark window as if trying to see into the future. "What about you and Susan, Fox? Any spark left there?"

"Not on her part," Edley said. "She's changed so much I don't even know her, and she don't even want to know me. Didn't expect her to be in love with me, but I thought she might still *like* me a little."

"She's a difficult woman to read." Travers laughed with gentle irony. "But they all are, for that matter. An eternal mystery to man. I wish Priscilla had married, instead of waiting. I guess Lash wishes the same about Karen Lindley.''

"Not many gals'd wait like that." Edley spat with accuracy. "But they wouldn't have men like you and Lash to wait for, a course. Think I was cut out to stay single. Always be a wild hoss.''

"The right lady could break you, Foxcroft.''

Edley guffawed. "There ain't no such animal, Milton the Third.''

Travers glanced up from scanning some papers Fox had done. "How'd you learn to read and write so well? You say you never went to school.''

"My ma taught me," Fox Edley said proudly. "Just a saloon girl, she hadda do somethin to support me, but she was smart. Taught me readin and writin an 'rithmetic. My father was British, an Oxford graduate, Ma told me. I never saw him. Too bad I couldn't a inherited some of his brains. But he was a bad one, a no-good drifter, all charm and no guts.''

"You've done all right, Fox," said Travers.

"Well, thanks to Ma, and you and Lash, I ain't done too bad." Edley agreed bashfully. "There are worse hombres around. Specially in El Paso and Juarez.''

"The crime wave has slowed to a ripple anyway, I don't quite know why or how." Travers pulled out a silver flask and poured two drinks into tall clean glasses, handing one to the Fox. "All we have to do is bust the big men at the top.''

"How we goin to swing it?''

Travers grinned. "We may have to shoot up city hall before we're through, Fox." He was sealing envelopes now.

"That'll be a great pleasure, Trav," said Edley. "Lemme help with them envelopes. Remember the buffalo hunters on the Staked Plains? I got to thinkin of 'em tonight, for some reason. Wyatt Earp, Jack Bridges, Pat Garrett, Bat Masterson, and the rest."

"Yeah, they're all big names up in Kansas and thereabouts in recent years. Immortalized by Ned Buntline."

"No bigger than we are in Texas," declared Fox Edley.

"That's right, pard." Travers pressed the flap on a final envelope and sighed in relief. "That does it for tonight, Fox. Let's seek refreshment in some nice quiet saloon."

"A noble idea. Ben Dowell's joint, for instance."

They drained their glasses, put on hats and jackets, snuffed out the lamps, left the office, and locked the door.

Outside it was snowing lightly in the mild night, and the plaza was ringed with vari-colored lamps, amber and pink, blue and green. Hitchrails were crowded, but few people or vehicles were on the move. A slow breeze from the pass swirled snowflakes and brought the howling of wolves and coyotes, the bark of dogs, and faint strains of music.

"Let's see if Red Bush is back at the Franklin," suggested Fox Edley.

Travers started to reply and crumpled suddenly. Fox heard the bullet strike Trav as he opened his own jacket to draw and fire at the fading muzzle flash between two stores across the way. Travers was down on the slatted walk, and Edley dropped beside him, a second slug searing past them to screech off adobe bricks. Edley threw another shot into that alley mouth, and saw the dark figure rock and twirl, nearly falling before staggering away into the blackness. Tagged that bushwhackin bastard, Fox thought.

"You're hit, Trav," he said, with anxiety.

"Not bad. Go after him, Fox. I'm all right."

"I can't leave you."

Travers got to his feet unaided, left arm pressed to his side, and Edley rose from his knees. "Go after the sonofabitch, Fox!" he ordered harshly. "I'm okay, I can walk, it's nothing. Don't let the bastard get away, for chrisake!"

Travers leaned back on the mud-brick wall, and waved Edley away with a savage gesture of his right hand, which now held a Colt. "Get going, goddamn it!"

Reluctantly, Fox Edley left him and ran bowlegged across the plaza for that alley. Glancing back over his left shoulder, Fox saw Travers beckoning and yelling at a man driving past on a buckboard. The horse and wagon stopped, and Fox knew Trav had a ride to the doctor's or the hospital. Couldn't be hit too hard, the way he got up and yelled at Edley.

A vague light in the rear area showed the alleyway to be clear, and Fox Edley raced through it. The sniper had been hit, and left a spattered trace of blood drops. Edley followed them across a backyard, expecting a gun to explode in his face any second. The man couldn't be far ahead. Edley heard the scrambling sounds of his slow progress.

The snow had increased enough to coat the ground thinly, and it was easy to follow the blood spoor on the whiteness, even in the dim light. It led through alleys and backlots, under peach trees and poplars, cedars and chinaberries. Edley was sweating and the snowflakes cooled his hot face. At every corner he anticipated a gunblast that would rip his head off, but he went grimly on following the erratic zigzag trail of scattered blood spots, dark on the new snow. At last he had a chance to gun down one of the enemy, and he didn't intend to lose it. He had wounded the man at long range, and he was closing in for the kill. Edley plodded onward, panting, slipping in the snow, Colt hanging in his right hand.

The shot came as he rounded the corner of a horse

shed, the lead *cracking* past his right ear, the flame almost blinding him. It was Fasaro, wiry and dapper, silver conchas gleaming palely on his heavy braided jacket, white teeth shining under his thin mustache. The tiny bells on his peaked sombrero chimed faintly, as he leaned swaying on a post, midway of the shed. *One of the big ones,* Fox thought exultantly.

Fox Edley whipped his gun up into line with fluid quickness and fire burst from it on a level trajectory, smashing Fasaro against the wooden upright. Bent in the middle, tottering on splayed feet, Fasaro's pistol blazed on a down-slant, and dirt sprayed Edley's boots. Fox waited a moment while Fasaro strove vainly to straighten up and lift his gunhand.

"You're under arrest," Edley said. "Leggo of the gun."

"You Rangers—don't take prisoners," Fasaro panted out, propped on the post. "Finish it—man."

"Who killed Rube Caldwell?"

"Not me, man. Ask—his—wife."

"Who's she in love with?"

"Again—not me—unfortunately."

"It's Hook Cano, isn't it?"

"Much man—with women. Ask Señora Caldwell." Fasaro managed a sneer, and his gun jerked upward.

Fox Edley shot him through the middle. Fasaro sagged and slid to earth in a seated posture, back to the post, legs sticking out in front of him. With a grunted gasp the Mex drew up his knees, toppled sideways from the upright, stiffened out, and was still on the snowy ground.

Edley forced himself to move forward, make sure of his victim, and search the body. He came up with a pouchful of money, but no papers of any kind, no more information. Fox reloaded, left the dead man there, and walked toward the nearest lighted street.

He had to find where Travers had gone, and see how bad he was hurt. He hoped the wound was as slight as it had seemed. Even so, it would keep Trav out of action for a time. Fox Edley decided he'd go to Susan Caldwell and ask her flat-out about Hook Cano. With all that smoke, there must be some fire. Fox was almost certain now that Hook Cano was Susan's lover, and that together they had murdered Rube Caldwell and contrived to make it appear like suicide. How could she do it, with those nice kids?

Lash said once that two people could have done it. Those were the two, without a shred of doubt. Fox Edley hated to admit it, but there seemed no alternative. The woman he had once held above all others was a traitorous killer, the *puta* of Hook Cano. How could a woman sink to such depths?

"Jesus Christ," Fox Edley murmured to himself. "What an ungodly mess. Rube's lucky to be out of it."

Maybe we can rid him of the taint of suicide, at least, Fox Edley thought. It won't help Rube any, but it'll clear his name. And perhaps grant his family more insurance. Leave his name untarnished in Ranger records. It wasn't much, but it was the best they could do.

I wonder if I can face Susan, without throwing up? Edley thought, sick in mind and heart. I wonder if I could bring myself to shoot her down, as she deserves? Probably not, but I'll see that she pays in full, somehow or other. All that she owes, and that is her life.

SEVENTEEN

Since Rube's death, Susan Caldwell could no longer stand herself and her life without drinking daily. She needed the alcohol to numb her against the horror that life had become. She developed a high resistance to booze and an enormous capacity. She drank all day but never got drunk. Susan felt she no more belonged to the world, to the children, to anyone. Except *him*. She lived solely for him.

Losing all patience with the children, she curtailed the daily lessons and sent them out to play, no matter how bad the weather was. She still got their meals on a fairly regular basis, washed the dishes, made the kids bathe, and kept their clothes clean. But her remoteness frightened them. They couldn't get close to her, find comfort and consolation in her. She wasn't really there anymore.

He sent Mex riders to deliver groceries, liquor, and all the fundamental necessities, and to run errands for her, paying for everything himself. He came to her in a closed carriage or small hooded supply wagon, and sent a nurse to watch the children when she went to his place in one or other of those vehicles. Thank God for the telephone, although Susan knew the operators must do a lot of talking. Their gossip didn't reach anyone of importance, Susan assumed.

It had been love at first sight, even though they met unromantically enough in the waiting room of a dentist. Susan was dazzled. She had never seen a man so handsome, gallant, and supremely sure of himself. In his closed carriage, he took her to a small cantina in the Mexican quarter, the *barrio* of El Paso. He had an easy, pleasant way with people, and was admired and respected everywhere. Feared also, she imagined. That was the beginning. The entire world changed for both of them.

Susan was completely enslaved from the start. If she felt any guilt, it was on account of the children and not her husband. She had long ago yielded Rube to his work. They occupied separate rooms and seldom had anything to say to one another. As the situation worsened, Rube even lost interest in the children. She never should have married him anyway. He was too dull, sober, and serious for her, no fun or laughter or romance in him. Fox Edley would have been a better mate. But after seeing this man, Susan knew there was nobody else on earth for her.

She tried to be nice to the kids, but constant drinking eroded her patience and flayed her nerves. When little Peter asked why there were so many greasers around all the time, she cuffed his head. When Reuben, Junior, told her she drank too much, she slapped his cheek with resounding force. Mary Ann, the youngest, cried and wailed all the time nowadays. Susan could not soothe and restore the pretty little girl. All her attention and love went to the man.

They fought, as savagely as they made love, but that was to be expected where emotions were so highly

167

charged. He was jealous and suspicious, as if she made a practice of betraying her man, when as a fact she had never even considered being unfaithful to Rube before this occurred. Although Rube lost all interest in her, Susan had remained true and steadfast. But on meeting this marvelous man, she was swept helplessly away. She'd never dreamed there were lovers like him. He took her to heights of rapture she'd only fantasized in the past.

Not many people had telephones yet. When theirs was first installed, the neighbors were always asking to use it, but Rube had put a stop to that. And Susan had frozen them out finally, after they'd been considerate and generous in their sympathy at the time of Rube's death. She couldn't have friends running in and out, and maintain her relation with the man she loved beyond all natural bounds. She didn't care to see anybody but him. Susan needed him more than she did air or water or food—or even liquor.

The kids were morosely unhappy these days. The light had gone out of their eyes and faces, and no more childish laughter echoed in the halls. They felt unloved, unwanted, abandoned, and alone in a large and terrifying world. Susan's heart ached, but she had nothing left to give them. The man took everything, every last ounce in her being. She lived only for their secret moments together.

Of late he was growing more and more jealous, almost insanely so. They quarreled viciously, and then made love in the same fashion, as if bent on destroying one another. He accused her of being intimate with Fox Edley, with Lashtrow, with Travers.

"For the love of God, do you think I'm a common whore?" Sue demanded.

"I can't endure the thought of another man having

you," he said. "I'll kill you if you ever let another man touch you."

"You have nothing to worry about, darling. I don't want anyone else to touch me—not ever. Can't you see that I love you to distraction?"

"You're very sensual, very sexual. In nightmares I see you in the arms of other men. I wish you wouldn't drink so much, Susie."

"I have to drink now, goddamn it! And you know why."

"It's dangerous though, Sue. Those Rangers come here anytime they want. One of them might catch you drunk, and—"

"I never get drunk," she said coldly.

"Anyone who drinks that much gets drunk, sooner or later. Drunk and helpless. If it ever happens, I'll kill you and the man both."

"If you're that possessive, you might marry me."

"I'm going to, for chrisake. After a decent time passes, and things get cleared up and straightened out in The Pass."

Susan laughed. "Be a helluva long time before that comes about, sweet."

"It won't be that long," he promised. "All we have to do is kill a few goddamn Rangers."

"Or be killed by them. These Rangers are the best shootists in the whole outfit, you know."

"You think I can't take them? You think I'm not better than they are? No man alive can beat me with a gun. Not even Lashtrow or Travers. Certainly not Bouchard or Edley."

Susan laughed. "Don't forget young Rammel."

Snarling, he struck her sharply on the side of the head. She broke into tears, and he clasped her in his muscular arms. Moments later they were back in bed.

That's the way it went with them, fighting and loving.

"Sometimes I think there are only two things you like to do," he told her, laughingly. "They both begin with the same letter."

"You're an evil wicked man."

"That's why you love me, *cara mia.*"

"One reason, perhaps," she admitted.

He was some kind of man, all right. Acting and looking as if he owned the earth and everyone on it. Handsome, arrogant, the devil incarnate in his brilliant eyes and merry smile, every move graceful, exuding charm and power and superb confidence. Daring and reckless, yet cool and controlled, serene in his strength of mind and body. A great fighter, a great lover, always in command.

Only Lashtrow, and perhaps Travers, could come anywhere near to matching him, and by her standards they fell far short. But they worried her. They'd had more experience than this man of hers. For many years they'd faced and beaten the top gunmen. But they'd never take *him.* He was indomitable, the king of the hill, master of all he surveyed, the world's greatest. No one could stand against him. Few would dare to try.

Lash and Trav would, of course. Likewise the Fox and Red Bush. Those four left a chill thread of fear in the back of her mind.

"You're worried," he accused. "You think they're better than I am?"

"Never, my darling." She smiled adoringly at him. "I know you're the very best. The top *pistolero* of all time, my sweet."

They sat on the edge of the bed and sipped Napoleon cognac.

"The new sheriff, Drumm, is working in fine. Kriewold was too damn cantankerous and unpredictable. But Drumm'll do all right."

"Did you kill Kriewold?"

"Of course not, I told you before. I don't even know how he died."

"I just had the notion you shot him."

"Why should I? He was on our side. Not much help maybe, but still on our side. Nobody seems to know who killed him."

"I'll bet *you* know."

"I don't know everything. Not quite. What the hell difference does it make, Susie?"

"None. Just a woman's curiosity, I guess."

He got up and began dressing, after a glance at his gold watch. "I've got to be getting back downtown."

Like all men, she thought wistfully. Once the act is consummated they want to get back to the world of business and action. "Must you go already?" How many times had she said that to him? She started putting on her own clothes, a simpler task than his, since she'd been prepared for his visit. She sighed, dreading the lonely hours ahead.

"I don't want to go. I have to. You know that." He was in a hurry now.

They were at her house, in the secret basement room she had rigged up with great care. The children were outside playing, their thin shouts heard faintly now and then. Even Rube hadn't known of this cellar room. He hadn't been home enough to know much about the house.

"I'll call the kids in the front way upstairs," Susan said, unnecessarily.

"I know, I've been here before," he said irritably, slipping into his rich leather jacket, cocking the hat on his sleek head. "I'll call you." He kissed her goodbye and turned to the short stairway leading up to the bulkhead at the rear.

"When, dearest?" she called after him.

"Soon as I can." His tone was impatient. "You better not phone me."

"Don't fret, I won't," Susan said flatly.

Upstairs she poured another drink before calling the children. Chancing to catch a glimpse of herself in a gilt-framed mirror, Susan was horrified. She looked like she felt, falling apart, crumbling to pieces, a slovenly dissipated young hag, beginning to show age. My God! He won't be coming around too often, if I go on looking like this. Got to brace up, snap out of it, start taking care of myself again.

Resisting the impulse to smash her glass against the mirror, Susan went to the front door to summon the kids in for their midafternoon snack. Poor dear little critters, she thought, fighting back tears. Born into a crazy hellhole of a world they never asked for. Father dead, and mother worse than dead. God bless 'em and care for 'em. Their bitch of a mother can't seem to help them anymore, full of booze and lust and hopeless despair, guilt and shame and heartbreaking sorrow.

God help the children: Reuben, Junior, and Peter and tiny Mary Ann.

How they love Lashtrow, she thought. He liked and played and laughed with them. My man doesn't even know they exist, except as nuisances. And what about me? Oh God in heaven, I ought to do away with myself. The kids would be better off without me. I'm not fit to live.

EIGHTEEN

"Why the hell you doin this?" asked the barber. "You got a beautiful beard there." He regarded the shining russet beard with open admiration.

"Maybe I wanta see what I look like," Rusty Bouchard said solemnly.

"You're apt to be disappointed." The barber laughed at his witticism.

"I've steeled myself against that. I just gotta find out the awful truth."

"Must be a better reason, Red."

"Well, I gotta new woman who hates beards."

The barber grunted. "That's more like it. But you're goin to be sorry. A beard like that!"

"I expect to have some regrets," Bouchard admitted. "But it's got to go. It'll grow back—in time."

"Be a helluva lot easier to change girls." The barber was in rare form today, and fully appreciative of his own humor.

"Go to work, goddamn it." Bouchard shifted in the chair, and rolled his broad powerful shoulder. "I ain't got all day."

"Yes, sir." The barber sobered. "But I gotta warn yuh, it's goin to be a long job."

"Just so it's a good one."

"You want the hair cut, too?"

"Close and short."

The man clicked his shears and sighed, regarding the rich wavy copper-red hair as if it were an art work he'd been ordered to destroy.

"You're a barber, ain't you?" Bouchard said. "Start cuttin, for chrisake."

"You're goin to look terrible, mister."

"That's my worry," Bouchard said. "Don't cry over it. Just go to work."

It was a monumental operation. The tonsorial artist finally got the hair short enough to suit Red Bush, and then had to trim the luxuriant beard down before shaving it. Bouchard lay back in comfort with his eyes shut, calm and relaxed. The stove in the corner radiated heat, and the little barber was sweating profusely.

When it was over at last, Bouchard sat up and stared at a bare pale-faced stranger in the glass, feeling and looking naked as a jaybird. It was a square ugly face, craggy, hacked roughly out of stone, relieved only by the velvet-brown eyes and the wide pleasant mouth. The upper part was weathered to deep bronze, the lower portion fishbelly white.

"Christ on the cross," Bouchard murmured. "Put the beard back on."

"I told yuh," said the barber triumphantly.

"Well, it could be worse," Red Bush said, with mild venom. "I coulda looked like you, I s'pose."

The barber laughed feebly, nervously. "You satisfied, sir? I did the best I could."

"You done good enough. I'll get used to it after a while." Bouchard climbed out of the chair, still gazing in fascination at the mirror. "Would you recognize me as

174

the man who came in here?"

"Never in christ's world!" declared the barber. "Your best friends won't know you. Your woman'll never believe it's you."

"Fine, fine, that's great," Red Bush said, a grin softening his two-toned rocky features. "How much I owe you?"

"Have to charge you a dollar for that job."

"Cheap enough." Bouchard laughed and handed him a dollar and a half. "You got anythin that'd darken my cheeks up a mite?"

"I got some salve I made up myself. Tenderfoots like to rub it on so they look suntanned. Only half a buck—for you, friend."

"Perfect!" Rusty paid him and examined the small tin of brown ointment.

"Here, lemme put it on for yuh. No sense gettin your hands all gooey." He applied the stuff with deft light fingers, and it was soothing to the raw skin. "See, it ain't too oily. It blends right in nice. I soak the city dudes two or three bucks a can." Finished he gave Rusty the tin and wiped his hands on a towel.

Bouchard inspected his new face with care in the looking-glass. "Hey, that's a lot better and I don't feel so damn naked. That's all right." It did make a large improvement, converting his face to one color, at least. "I'm obliged to you."

"Glad to help out. Come in again."

Bouchard strapped on his guns, tied down the sheaths, and got into his buffalo-hide jacket. "Hope it don't turn cold and freeze my bare face." Putting on his hat, he consulted the mirror once more, flipped a big paw at the proprietor, and walked out of the shop. He had kept a short-barreled pistol in his belt while in the chair.

The brown mustang he'd taken from the livery, in

case the Mexicans had spotted him on the big gray, was waiting at the hitchrack. The day was clear and fair, the last snow already melted off in the sun, but the air felt icy on his shaved cheeks and neck. The feeling of nakedness persisted.

It had been a considerable sacrifice to part with the beard, but it was too dangerous to prowl around Juarez with those red whiskers marking him as the Ranger gunny who had shot Quadah in the Franklin Hotel saloon. Bouchard now wanted Hook Cano, as bad as he had wanted Quadah. The Injun had murdered Lily Lavoy on orders from Cano, he was certain, and he felt sure Hook was hiding out across the river. Beardless, Bouchard could move freely about and track down the bastard in Juarez. Catch him alone and kill him. Getting the Hook had been an obsession with Red Bush, ever since the Apache had slaughtered poor sweet Lily Lavoy. He'd never rest easy until Hook Cano was dead.

With the beard shaved off, Bouchard had expected to feel practically invisible, a ghost moving unseen about old familiar places. Instead he felt more conspicuous than ever, as if everyone on the street was looking at, into and through him. He was exposed and vulnerable as never before, strange and weak, like Samson shorn of his hair and strength. It left him bewildered and uncertain, but he urged the brown bronc on toward the main bridge connecting El Paso to Juarez. On previous occasions he had used the lesser bridges or forded the Rio Grande.

The officers at the Border Patrol station knew Bouchard, but passed him by without recognition. He'd wanted to test his appearance there, and was encouraged, as he clopped on across the bridgeway above the muddy stream. At the other end, some of the Mexican officers knew Bouchard, by sight at least, but revealed no signs of it as they admitted him with bored indifference to Juarez and Mexican territory. There was so much traffic daily and nightly that the officials on both sides had become lax and careless. It was inevitable, Red Bush supposed.

The crimes against American citizens had dwindled down to nothing, of late, for no discernible reason. It must be that Hook Cano was getting a bit shorthanded, having lost some of his tophands and sent a large crew off with the stolen Anvil herd. The Anvil cowboys, Arizona and Val Verde, had slain two rustlers up in the Sacramentos. Rammel was reported to have killed two or three in Pinon, New Mexico. In El Paso, Travers had cut down Reboza, and last night Fox Edley had blasted Fasaro. Red Bush himself had put away Quadah, of course. Hook Cano must be hurting bad.

Milt Travers was in the hospital with a bullet graze in his left side, but no bones had been nicked and Trav would be up and around fairly soon. It would have been hell if Trav had gone under, when he was about ready to resign, go home to Boston, marry Priscilla Cabot, and settle down to a writing career. Things often happened that way in this cockeyed, screwed-up world. Thank the Lord fate and a few inches had spared Milt's life this time. Humanity couldn't afford to lose a man like Travers.

On earlier excursions to Juarez, Bouchard had been a living target, with hostile dark eyes following that fiery beard wherever he went. Today he was anonymous and nobody paid any attention to him, as he jogged aimlessly around the Mexican settlement with its ancient adobes and blank-faced missions. Gradually he began to attain the security he had anticipated with his beard gone. He was just another gringo drifter in dirty, sweated, hardworn range garb, on a nondescript brown nag.

In the past Bouchard had observed that *El Con-*

177

quistador seemed to be the favorite hangout of the *bandidos*. He hadn't seen Hook Cano, but all the others were in and about there quite often. Rusty remembered when the one-legged outlaw, Chichi Chavez, had owned the place, and had vainly sought to learn the name of the present owner. No one seemed to know, or if they did were not telling. A breed called Fat Angelo was the manager.

It was the largest and best cantina in town, a long two-story structure of whitewashed adobe bricks, a gallery extending the length of the facade, the hitchrail always lined with saddle horses, buggies, wagons, and buckboards. The ground floor was occupied by a saloon at the left, and a restaurant on the right. There must be many slit-windowed rooms upstairs, most of them used by the house girls to entertain clients, no doubt.

With his beard like a flaunted red flag to local *pistoleros*, famous since his killing of Quadah across the river, Bouchard never had been foolhardy enough to venture into the cantina, but today or tonight he would make an entrance. For the present he reclined on a box in the shade of a board-awninged little shop across the street, shoulders against the wall, hat tipped over brown eyes, bowlegs stretched before him. He puffed on a long cigar, and drank at intervals from a large bottle of beer, watching the customers flow in and out of *El Conquistador*.

It was time for Lashtrow and the Anvil crew to be coming back with Ashley's cattle. Bouchard had such confidence and faith in Lash he never doubted they'd recover the herd, and drive it back to Yeager's Stockyard in El Paso. When he saw a smudge of dust to the south, he was positive it was made by the returning cows and steers, He wondered if Fox Edley was actually going to confront Susan Caldwell with accusations about her relationship with Hook Cano. It would be a painful ordeal for the Fox, but he was the logical man to do it.

Bouchard had been suspicious of Susan almost from the start, but he hadn't said anything out of deference to Edley. Lash and Trav shared his feelings, but none of them wanted to hurt Fox Edley. Red Bush knew that women, good and bad, were capable of anything when caught in the throes of emotion. He thought of Lily Lavoy with a deep pang of loss and sorrow. Lily might have been a whore, but she was a woman to trust. *We sure get a lot of good people killed.* Lily had been murdered because of her association with himself and Lash—and Rube Caldwell.

Things were coming to a head now. If he could take Hook Cano, that would break up the renegade bunch. Then they'd go after the bastards in city hall. That's where the evil emanated from. Good thing somebody had knocked off Kriewold, but the new sheriff, Drumm, was said to be even worse. So far as Bouchard knew, Kriewold and Drumm were the only two dangerous gunslingers among the big moguls of El Paso, although Fribance and Yeager were rated by some as fairly good with the irons.

Rammel ought to be pulling in from New Mexico before long, and they'd need him for the showdown, with Travers out of action temporarily. Ram sure cut a swath for himself up in Pinon. One of these days that boy's going to be fastest gun in the Rangers, which means in Texas or the whole Southwest. When Lash and Trav slow a split-second, Ram'll be the top. *I hope to christ he and Lash never square off, but it may come someday.*

Bouchard recalled the first time he'd laid eyes on Milton Travers up in the Indian Nations. Red Bush had been living there as a hermit, after the death of Singing Bird, friend of the Osages, killing Apaches as fast as possible. Dressed in clean new buckskins given him by old Chief Gray Eagle, a Confederate forage cap on his fair head, mounted on a coyote dun, Milt Travers had ridden up to Bouchard's cabin at the head of an Osage war party, on the trail of Apaches.

Bouchard had joined them, and after a battle with Apaches they had rescued Lashtrow and Tess Hiller from a dugout, in which they'd been pinned down by Deke Vennis's outlaw band. At that time Rammel was riding with Vennis. Red Bush had taken to Travers, Lashtrow, and the girl Tess, right from the start, and to Rammel when he came over to their side soon after. They had helped Anse Amidon finish his trail drive up the Chisholm to Abilene. Rammel and Tess Hiller had fallen in love and married.

That fall Bouchard and Rammel had signed on with the Rangers, largely on account of Lashtrow and Travers. At headquarters in Austin they had met Foxcroft Edley, third member of the legendary Ranger triumvirate. The Three Musketeers had soon become the Big Five.

Bouchard put aside his fond memories to face the present, as winter dusk closed in. Soon it would be time for him to enter *El Conquistador*. His hunch was that Hook Cano had secret quarters on that second floor, and Red Bush had to get upstairs and make sure. It was a long shot but he was bent on doing it. He had to get Hook Cano, before Lily Lavoy could rest peacefully in her grave. Or he could live at peace with himself.

Tall, light-skinned Tatum and squat dark Pablito had been going to and fro all afternoon at *El Conquistador*. They were the only two Bouchard recognized, but Hook must have recruited replacements for Quadah, Fasaro and other lieutenants. There'd be enough of them to make it interesting, Red Bush reflected ironically.

As lamps began to blossom through the dust and haze, Bouchard took a stroll to loosen his muscles. Laughter and music floated from cantinas and homes, mission bells tolled in the murky air, and spicy cooking scented the streets. The wind rustled in leafless poplar, tupelo, and pepper trees, and soapweed seeds clacked in withered pods. Once again Bouchard felt all the spectral mystic qualities of Old Mexico press in on him. A paradoxical race: proud and humble, noble and base, brave and cowardly, generous and selfish, romantic and practical, kind and cruel.

Completing a circuit Bouchard ambled into the wide, glass-doored entrance of *El Conquistador*, where gay music lilted through blue layers of tobacco smoke. It was elaborate, clean, and well-kept. An adobe partition with a central archway separated the saloon and eating room. The long mahogany bar and mirror, the brass lamps and fixtures, were polished to a high sheen. Dark pretty girls in white silk dresses moved among the tables, flaunting their figures and flirting their eyes.

To Rusty's surprise, Fat Angelo came forward to greet him, an immense man in immaculate clothing with a broad jolly face and beaming smile under lacquered black hair. He extended a fat heavy hand, and Rusty was surprised again at the strength of it.

"Ah, a new customer, señor. Welcome to our place. Make it your home and enjoy yourself." Angelo led him to a small central table and summoned a waiter. Bouchard ordered a bottle of Spanish brancy and an *olla* of water. A slim vivacious girl appeared at his elbow. "Our loveliest señorita," Fat Angelo said, moving away as Rusty invited her to sit down.

They clicked glasses and exchanged pleasantries, the

girl speaking in perfect English with an exquisite accent. She was a true Latin beauty, and he wondered why Fat Angelo lavished so much hospitality on him. It had to mean he was under strict surveillance. But the girl was a necessity.

Bouchard had to get upstairs. The only way was with a señorita.

"My name is Miranda," she said. "What do I call you, señor?"

"The name is almost as pretty as you. Just call me Red."

She glanced at his cropped head and nodded. "Do you sometimes wear a beard?"

Bouchard laughed to cover his discomfort. "Once in a while, when I'm too lazy to shave. I got a face that needs coverin up."

"Oh, no!" Miranda cried softly. "You have a nice strong man's face."

"*Gracias,* but I know I got the kinda looks that require a lotta personality to make up for."

Miranda laughed, a ripple of music. "I can tell you have that—Red."

"I try," Bouchard said modestly, brain busy. He didn't really want a woman, even one as desirable as this, but it was the only way to reach the second floor. His mind was still too full of Lily Lavoy—and Hook Cano—to lust after another girl. Or maybe he was simply growing old in his late thirties. The hell he was.

Well, there was no hurry. Miranda was well versed in her trade, making a man feel comfortably at home, flattering him with eyes and voice, displaying interest in his conversation, complementing it with her own. She wore a sensuous perfume that penetrated subtly through the cognac. Her face was fine Castilian, her body slender but lushly ripe, with that enchanting depth at breast and hip. Fat Angelo had chosen well for him. Bouchard wished this opportunity had arisen in better circumstances.

Of course Red Bush comprehended that Miranda had been delegated to find out who and what he actually was, and why he was there. But she wasn't likely to accomplish that. He saw the stairway at the rear beside the dividing wall, with frequent couples climbing or descending. Business was brisk all around, at the bar, in the restaurant, and upstairs. He couldn't keep Miranda idle for any great length of time.

They had become friends when they ascended the stairs, with the bottle in the jacket pocket, thrown over his left arm. He was aware of many eyes on them, but Miranda's figure might account for that. Delectable in her flawless white gown that fitted tightly. The landing at the top opened into an entry hall, through the only visible break in the adobe partition. Double corridors with closed doors on either side extended ahead.

"What's on the other side, Miranda?" Bouchard nodded at the wall.

"I don't really know. I think Angelo lives there." Miranda took his right arm and guided him along the left-hand passage to her chamber.

It was roomier and better appointed than he had anticipated, a neat comfortable bedroom with a bureau, dressing table, easy chairs, ordinary table, and clothes closet. He had noticed the wider spaces on both sides of the door. Miranda was definitely Number One. The others probably used the cubicles he had expected.

The preliminaries over, they were naked in bed. Bouchard had slipped his short belly gun under the mattress when Miranda wasn't looking. The door crashed inward and open, startling them both, and Pablito was hunched there, silver-mounted pistol in hand, bulbous black eyes glaring ferociously above his flared nostrils and mean buck-toothed mouth.

"The fun is over, gringo. Get out, Miranda." Pablito flung a blue satin robe on the bed.

"For chrisake we haven't even started, man!" Bouchard said, rolling off the girl to the far side of the bed. "Are you crazy?"

"What are doing here, hombre?" demanded Miranda, sitting up with the sheet held over her breasts. "You have no right to break in on me."

"*El jefe* sent me, what the hell you think? Get outa here, Miranda. You don't wanta get blood all over, do yuh?"

She wriggled into the blue robe. "This is not my doing, Red. I knew nothing of this."

"It's all right, Miranda, I believe you," Bouchard said. "You'd better go, baby."

"Don't you kill him, damn your soul!" Dark eyes and classic features terror-stricken, Miranda fled the room, robe flying behind her. "I'll bring help, Red."

Pablito laughed and slammed the door shut. When he turned back to the bed, Bouchard had the gun under the sheet, which still covered him to the waist. He held it, cool and reassuring, beside his right knee.

"Thought you'd fool us by cutting off your beard, you red-headed sonofabitch?" Pablito jeered, holstering his pistol and drawing a knife. "To keep it quiet I'll use this, you gringo bastard!" He moved toward the bed, steel blade aglimmer in his low-held right hand. "I'll carve you up like a friggin turkey, Ranger!"

Rusty Bouchard cleared his gun and shot Pablito full in the face, jolting his head back, dropping him flat on his shoulderblades. Writhing and kicking briefly, Pablito sank into a motionless state, disbelief in his bulging eyes and shattered features.

Bouchard bounced from the bed and reached for his clothes draped on a chair. Suddenly the room seemed full of men with guns in hand, Tatum at the front of them, and saying, "Drop the iron, Red Bush!"

Turned half-away from them, Bouchard knew he had no chance, and for once let discretion prevail over senseless valor. He might die in a worse way later, but as long as a man was alive he had some chance, however meager. He loosed his fingers, let the stubby weapon fall to the floor, and drawled, "You mind if I put my pants on, amigos?"

From behind the ragged row of *pistoleros,* Hook Cano's voice rose loud and clear: "Don't shoot! Don't kill him. I wanta talk to the red-headed Ranger sonofabitch! Before he dies a little bit at a time, worse'n Quadah did, by jeezus."

"I got a refund comin here," Bouchard grumbled, getting into his clothing. "I paid for somethin I never got."

NINETEEN

The Anvil herd was back on Texas soil at last, ready for the homestretch drive up the Rio Grande valley to El Paso.

After recovering the cattle from that box canyon in the foothills of the Sierra Madre, where they left seven dead *bandidos*, they had laid over in Galeana, on the Rio de Ste. Maria River. The Mexican leader, Chacon, had been the only rustler to escape. Chappy and Rosita welcomed them back.

Lashtrow and Ashley were house guests of Chappy Chiapas, drinking themselves to sleep there. Cobb and Val Verde got drunk and slept in the hay loft of the livery barn. Arizona and Rosita Shaw disappeared and spent the night somewhere together. Chappy didn't like this, but he was too sophisticated to put the entire blame on Arizona. He knew his niece too well for that. The stock were in a holding pen at the edge of town.

In the gray-misted morning they buried Mullen, with Ashley conducting the simple graveside service, the men standing by with bare bowed heads and mournful eyes. Arizona made the ceremony with Rosita at his side.

Cobb and the girl were tearful. Dry-eyed, the others were no less grief-sticken. Mullen had been a good man, steady and quiet, easy-going, mild-mannered and solid as bedrock. They would all miss him, Cobb the most of all.

Ashley hired three *vaqueros*, recommended by Chiapas. Eight men were few enough to push a herd that now numbered about 1,500. Ashley also acquired a chuck wagon and a cook to drive it, which would serve for a bed-and-wood vehicle as well. The whole town of Galeana was out to see them start the long drive homeward. Band music made a carnival of it.

Rosita Shaw wanted to go with Arizona, but Chappy quickly and firmly disabused her of that fanciful notion.

The drive had gone well and without incidents, the weather remaining mild and clear. No more snowstorms and no attacks.

Several times groups of horsemen appeared in the distance, red men as well as brown or white, but they made no attempt at a raid. Quite possibly they had heard about the massacred rustlers and decided to keep their distance rather than face the *Americano* guns.

The drovers kept a moderate pace, giving the cattle time to graze and water where the buffalo grass was good, and never pushing them too hard. Men and beasts alike were gaunt, weary, and trailworn.

They stopped at the Potasi homestead briefly to greet the family that had granted them lifesaving hospitality during the blizzard, and Ashley left them a couple of cows gone lame. The Potasis were overwhelmed by a gift of such magnitude, but Ashley insisted that those two critters were slowing the drive and he was happy to be rid of them, glad they might be of use to his friends and benefactors. The Mexes showered thanks and blessings on him.

Mullen was sorely missed by all, and in particular by his long-time pardner Cobb. At odd moments, Lashtrow caught himself lookkng about for the good-natured Mully, with that shy grin creasing his red cheeks and lighting his sun-squinted eyes. To Cobb's knowledge, Mullen had no family.

The last news they'd had from El Paso, brought by Chappy's niece Rosita Shaw, was that Lily Lavoy had been chopped up by Quadah, and Red Bush had blown the Injun apart in retaliation. With a lot of time to think in the dry winter dust of the drive, Lashtrow had been pondering on Hook Cano's hiding place.

In the old days *El Conquistador Cantina* had been owned by a part-time outlaw and badman, Chichi Chavez, whom Lash had cause to remember well. One night far down-river in Laredo, Lashtrow was drinking in a high-class saloon, The Madrid, where you had to check your guns on entry. He'd been at the far bend of the bar, when Chavez came in with his beloved shotgun and lined it at Lash. He'd have been a dead man, if the barkeeper hadn't tossed him a stubby shotgun. Lash caught it and dove aside, as Chichi's weapon flamed thunderously. Firing from the floor, Lash's charge had nearly torn a leg off Chavez, knocking him down and out. They had to amputate, and thereafter Chichi Chavez stumped around on a wooden leg, vowing that he would someday blow both legs off Lashtrow. He never got the opportunity, and wound up dead under Rammel's gun, when they were working the Butterfield Stagecoach Line case in El Paso.

The point was that Chief Calderon and his outlaw crew had used *El Conquistador* as an in-town hideout in those days, and Hook Cano might be doing the same at present. It was worth a try, at any rate.

Now, having helped punch the Anvil herd across the

shallows of the Rio Grande, Lashtrow told Ashley he was going to play a hunch, recross to Mexico, and ride up that side of the river to enter Juarez by the back door, so to speak. It was only a few miles to the Yeager Stock-yard in El Paso, and they could easily complete the drive without him.

Ashley thanked Lash for everything and they shook hands, agreeing to see one another soon at The Pass.

Arizona called, "You must like it over there, Lash. Just keep clear of my gal Rosita."

"Only going to Juarez, kid."

Val Verde smiled and waved soberly, and Cobb merely raised a huge hand. The Cobber spoke but rarely to anyone, since the loss of Mullen.

Lashtrow splashed back across the Rio Grande, and turned north up the Mexican side, soon leaving the dust of the cattle behind.

The sun was dipping redly behind the Hatchet Mountains, turning the western horizon into a wilderness of changing colors, and on the plain shadows were lengthening gray and blue, lavender and purple, with a short-lived rosy tinge that faded as the sun sank out of sight.

Lashtrow seemed to remember vaguely a good-looking kid named Cano, a hanger-on in the bandit fringe that frequented *El Conquistador*. Unknown then but already beginning to build a reputation with a gun, a reckless, merry, go-to-hell boy with a handsome smiling face and laughing brown eyes. That was before he lost his right hand, and gained fame for his lightning left-hand draw. Hook Cano, daring desperado, hero to Mexican youth, glamorous idol of the señoritas, a killer with an impressive list of victims. Too young to join the Calderon gang, he was soon leading a bunch of his own, surpassing the quiet gentlemanly Calderon in notoriety.

Even though he'd had to kill him, Lashtrow always thought of Chief Calderon with respect—and regret. A fine man on the wrong side of the law. I could have gone that outlaw route myself, Lash knew. If Ranger Captain Cactus Bill McKenna hadn't found me and turned me around. In turn Fox Edley and Aubrey Rammel actually were bad men, until Lash and Travers converted them. The line dividing good and bad was extremely thin on the frontier.

The azure-hazed winter dusk thickened to black, and the lights of Juarez twinkled ahead. Lashtrow booted his hammer-headed bronc forward, and thought of his great sorrel penned up in Yeager's stable. He hoped Amanda Ashley had been exercising the golden horse, as he had requested of her. He was certain she had, for Amanda was a very reliable and obliging woman. Ash was lucky in that respect, if unlucky with his stock.

In the overall picture, a good wife was more valuable than any herd of cattle. That set him to mooning, with wistful yearning, about Karen Lindley in San Antonio. And Trav's Priscilla Cabot in Boston. Two straight, true, long-waiting women, who deserved a better fate than loving a pair of Rangers. Great girls who'd likely end up alone.

It made Lash feel as sad as he did when thinking of his dead father, mother and maternal grandmother. That had been his family on the small Laurel Leaf spread near Uvalde, all gone now. Dad at Gettysburg in 1863, and the ladies not long afterward, leaving Alistair Lashtrow alone in a raw hostile world, to grow up fighting, first with fists, then guns.

Lash had liked working stock and the ranch with his father, and after a hot dust-eating day they would go swimming in the Nueces River or one of the creeks, and come out laughing and glowing clean. Everything was fun with big Dan Lashtrow. Then he had to go to war and get killed by the bluecoats on Cemetery Ridge, and nothing was ever quite the same after that, for Lash or the Confederacy.

He had no definite plan of action in Juarez, but one occurred to him as he surveyed the night time scene around *El Conquistador*, where business was booming. On the second floor were living quarters over the saloon, and at the other end above the restaurant, bell-like rooms in which the girls plied their trade. At the rear a loading platform ran the length of the whitewashed building, with back entrances to the barroom and café. Between them was a recessed doorway concealed behind shutters, probably opening on a stairway leading up to the apartments.

Diagonally across the street from the cantina front, about fifty yards distant, was a rickety open-faced wooden shed, a dubious shelter for horses and vagrants, empty at the moment. Mexicans loved fires. Lash would give them one to attend. A brisk blaze would bring most of the customers out of *El Conquistador*, and perhaps Hook Cano himself—or his bodyguards.

Lashtrow rode to the next parallel street, bought a can of kerosene, and cut through an alley to the rear of the horse shed. Splashing the wooden wall liberally with fuel, he set it afire and rode quickly out of the narrow passage to the street. Making a leisurely circuit, Lash saw people pouring out of the cantina and other places, as the flames leaped high to dim the stars. In the backyard he tied his bronc to a worn log rail, and waited in the shadow of the stable. Several men emerged shouting from the shuttered door and ran in the direction of the burning structure, excited and eager to form a bucket brigade or just to watch the blaze.

Lashtrow crossed the shadow-stippled yard and

climbed to the loading dock. In their drunken haste the greasers had left the shuttered gate open and the inner door unlocked. He opened the door carefully and mounted the staircase. At the top was a spacious littered room, centered by a round table under a hanging lamp, its surface strewn with playing cards among bottles and glasses. Charro jackets and *serapes* were slung over rawhide chairs, and two bunks occupied the far corners with a horsehair couch in between. Carbines were racked on the wall under a bracketed lamp.

The door to the right was ajar, revealing a richer, more elegant chamber with black leather armchairs and ornate tables. Peering in, Lash saw a battered flat desk at the far end, and beside it a bulky man trussed to a straight-backed wooden chair, his clean-shaven face bruised and blood-smeared, a pipe in his mouth. Evidently his hands had been left free to tend to the pipe. Beyond the desk Hook Cano stood slim and straight, back to the room, watching the fire through a window slit.

Lashtrow took a closer look at the seated prisoner, and his gray eyes widened. It was Rusty Bouchard, for chrisake, with his beard shaved off and his hair cut short, gazing dully at the carpeted floor. From the looks of it, they had worked Rusty over pretty good.

Quietly Lash stepped inside, without drawing. Bouchard glanced up and his rugged form jerked against the bonds, his welted brown eyes incredulous. With swollen lips he framed silent words: *Draw, for chrisake, draw*.

Hook Cano turned from the wall and masked his astonishment. "Lashtrow. How the hell—?" He was calm and unflustered. "Where are the goddamn guards?" He stood at languid ease, left hand near his low-hung gun.

Lashtrow grinned. "They went to the fire."

"I mighta known. You shoulda come ashootin, man. What you thinkin of?"

"I always wanted to see if that left hand was as good as they say."

"It'll cost you to find out. Just your life—and his." Cano moved forward to slouch easily on Bouchard's right side, a bit forward of him.

"I almost didn't know you, Red Bush," said Lashtrow.

"The perfect disguise backfired on me, Lash," Bouchard said sadly.

"*We* knew him. Tatum spotted him. Tatum's a smart hombre. But you was goddamn stupid to come in here without drawin, Lash."

"If I'd drawn I might've shot you in the back, Hook. Something I never wanta do." Lash's eyes were an intense green now.

"You'll wish to Christ you had!" There was no fear in Hook Cano.

"That remains to be seen," Lashtrow said. "You're all through here, Hook. Drop your belt and come with us. There's been enough killing."

Cano laughed in disdain. "We're in *Mexico,* Ranger! You can't take me here. Your badge ain't worth a *peso* in this country."

"Who's your boss, Hook?" Lash's face was windburned to Indian copper.

Cano laughed again. "I ain't got one. I'm the boss, Lash. I'm *numero uno.* You know that, for chrisake."

"You wanta die and let those hyenas in El Paso go free? Those city hall crumbs?" Lash's lips thinned into a straight severe line.

Cano waved his steel hook. "They won't last long. They're startin to shoot each other. Judge Milo

Bascomb killed Kriewold, the way I get it. Make your move, Lashtrow. Before my men get back." His left hand blurred into action like a striking snake.

Lash's draw was too fast to be seen, and his Colt came up blazing red. The bullet ripped into Hook's left arm, up near the shoulder, and spun him to the left, the pistol flying clear.

"Watch it, Lash!" Bouchard yelled, catching Cano's gun in mid-air and firing at the doorway, where Tatum had appeared with magical suddenness, his barrel trained on Lash's back. The slug smashed Tatum's chest and spoiled his aim, jarring him backward. Swiveling smoothly Lashtrow lined another shot into Tatum's body and sent him crashing to the floor.

Cano was leaping at Bouchard, the steel hook flashing toward Rusty's throat, when Lash whirled swiftly back and slashed a .44 into Cano's right side, flinging him across Bouchard's bound knees. Red Bush shoved him off, rolling on the carpet, and held the gun on him, but there was no call for another shot. Both bandits were unconscious, Tatum dead and Hook Cano dying. The room reverberated with the rapid explosions and powdersmoke sooted the air, stinging eyes and nostrils, rancid in their mouths.

"Come on, you beardless wonder." Lashtrow cut Bouchard loose from the chair, and they headed for the door, Red Bush stumbling on numbed bowlegs. "You got a horse over here, Rusty?"

"Yeah, if he ain't been stolen, Wolf."

They plunged recklessly down the stairs, out through the double doors to the platform, jumping to the ground, crossing to Lash's bronc. Bouchard climbed on behind him, and they found the brown cayuse still tethered where Rusty had left it on the other side of the street. Rusty swung down, grabbed the reins; up again to his own saddle, off and away after the fleeting Lashtrow. The shed was still burning behind them, a crowd of spectators milling around.

"Jeezus, that—happened fast," Bouchard said, panting as they circled toward the nearest ford in the Rio Grande.

"Where'd you learn—to pluck guns outa the air?" asked Lashtrow.

"Just one—a my special acts."

"Must've taken—a lotta practice."

"Years and years," Bouchard confessed. "You ain't slowed up any, Wolf."

They laughed as they rode, but they were still shaken, quivering inside.

"That oughta wind it up on this side of the border," Lashtrow said, as they reined to a trot.

"Yeah, the Cano bunch is outa business for dead sure," Bouchard agreed. "But the real big ones are still stinkin up the town hall on our side."

"They're the next item on the agenda, Red Bush," said Lashtrow.

"I was kinda glad to see you show back there, Lash. You bring the herd back okay?"

Lashtrow nodded. "Wiped out Chacon's crew, but he got away. Lost one of Ashley's riders, Mullen, a good man. What's new here, Red Bush?"

"The Fox blew Fasaro down last night. Trav's in the hospital with a flesh wound, nothin much. Ram ain't checked in yet. Kriewold's dead and buried. Hook claimed Bascomb done it, but I don't know. The judge ain't s'posed to be a gunsharp."

"How's Susan Caldwell?"

Bouchard shrugged. "About the same. On the bottle. She don't seem to want us around, but Foxcroft keeps goin back."

They slid their horses down a sandy bank into the water, and sloshed through the shallows to clamber out on the Texas shore, sighing in relief. Lash pulled a bottle out of his plunder, and they both drank from it. "You sure look funny without whiskers," Lash said, laughing.

The Anvil herd was bedded down in the stockyard, but in the Pueblo House lobby they found Amanda Ashley weeping softly.

"They arrested Ash and the boys, as soon as they got the stock penned up," she told them. "I didn't even get a chance to talk with Ash."

"What the hell for?" asked Lashtrow. "On what grounds, Amanda?"

"I don't know, Lash. Somebody said it was for stealing cattle."

"Their own herd, for the luvva christ?" rasped Bouchard. "Who done it?"

"That new sheriff, Drumm, with a posse of twenty deputies. Put them in a wagon and hauled 'em off to jail."

"They can't get away with that," Lash said. "They're crazy to try it. Don't worry, Amanda. We'll have 'em outa there in no time."

"You're damn right we will," Bouchard growled. "We'll roust that tinhorn sheriff and his egg-suckin deputies. Don't you fret a mite, ma'am. We'll bring 'em right back to yuh, quicker'n a wink."

"That's the ticket," said Lashtrow.

TWENTY

With more trepidation than usual, Fox Edley rode his blue roan up the sloping street toward the Caldwell home on the northern residential outskirts of El Paso. The night was still and cool, only a light breeze from the pass sighing through mulberry and manzanita branches, most of the houses dark and sleeping. The sky was an enormous canopy embroidered with frosty stars, the waning moon a tilted horn of gold amid a fleecy spindrift of clouds. Smoke rose from chimneys and nightbirds called on the misted heights.

Fox Edley confronted the hardest task of his life: Facing Susan Caldwell with a point-blank accusation about her relation with Hook Cano.

The red-brick house, behind its hedges and trees, was unlighted except for a faint glimmer from an inner room, the parlor, he guessed. Edley took the driveway to check out the patio and barn, the *grullo's* hooves slurring in the gravel. Moonbeams illuminated the back area. Nobody lurked there, but Fox saw fresh hoofprints running out alongside the stable. The back doors would be locked. He eased forward to dismount by the

front entrance on the gallery, gun still in hand, icy trem-
ors flickering up his backbone to tighten his scalp. Fox
sensed something wrong, some evil within the brick
walls. The spirit of Rube Caldwell seemed to hover in
the shadows.

No one came to answer his knock, and Fox's ap-
prehension grew. There was a dim light in the parlor,
he'd observed from the windows. He paced the porch,
more cluttered than ever with playthings: miniature
wagons and broncs, pails and shovels, dolls and trinkets,
sleds, hobby horses, and toy guns. Fox surveyed the
pitiful array with smarting eyes, wondering what would
become of young Rube, Peter, and Mary Ann, already
thinking of them as orphans. Fox was certain now of
Sue Caldwell's guilt.

Fox Edley dreaded to go inside, but it had to be done.
Turning back he tried the door, surprised when it
opened readily under his hand. He shut it quietly from
the inside and stood listening. The only sound was a low
moaning, as regular as breathing. On reluctant legs he
crept toward the living room, and his heart froze in his
chest as he reached the draped archway.

Sue Caldwell, her face ghastly, was lying back on a
doeskin lounge, both hands clasped to her body, beneath the high firm breasts that rose and fell with her
labored breath. Blood oozed through her fingers and
spread darkly on her gingham dress. Her black hair was
wildly disheveled, the gray eyes sunken in her drained
haggard face, lips colorless and dry. There was no taint
of gunsmoke. The sonofabitch had stabbed her, and
death was tangible in the room.

"Lemme look at that, Susan." He crossed to stand
over her.

"No use, Fox. I'm dying. A good thing—all around."

"I'll call the hospital."

"I already called—for the kids' sake."

"Where are they?" The lump in his throat made speaking difficult.

"Upstairs—asleep. Take care—of 'em, Fox. See that they're—taken care of." A groan of agony escaped her locked teeth.

"I will, Sue, don't worry." He knelt beside her. "Lemme see that wound."

"You can't—help me," she whispered faintly. "Nobody can. I'm done for. Can't live—don't wanta live . . . . But glad—you came, Fox. Knew you would. Stayed alive—waiting for you." Susan shuddered and squirmed in a rending spasm.

"Jesus Christ, can't I do *something?*" He'd never felt so helpless. "Get you something, Sue?"

"Nothing, Fox—not a thing." She tried to smile. "Not even—a drink."

Edley bowed his head, teeth grating. "You didn't—?"

"No, I didn't—stab myself. . . . Any more than—Rube shot himself."

Fox Edley stared at her. "It *was* murder then. Rube was murdered. I always figgered that. Who did it, Sue?"

"He did it—of course. With my help. God forgive me. I drugged him—and he shot him."

Edley gazed wonderingly at her, amber eyes and lean tough face mirroring his horror, throat too aching-full for words. He saw death in her eyes and face, very near now. *I was here that night,* he thought.

"Didn't know—he meant to—kill Rube," she panted brokenly. "Told me—he just wanted—him knocked out. So he could—go through—the files."

"Why'd he stab you, Sue?"

"Jealous—crazy jealous. Of you—and Lash—and Trav."

Fox Edley remained silent, dead and empty inside, his head twisting to and fro in mute anguish.

"Hate me. . . . Go ahead—hate me, Fox. You can't

hate me—half as much—as I hate myself. . . . Couldn't help it—I loved the man."

"I—I don't hate you, Susan," said Fox Edley, with an effort. "I—I'm just sorry—for you." Tenderly, he stroked her tousled feverish head.

"He thought—I was dead," she murmured, voice flat, hollow, lifeless. "But I had—to live—to see you—tell you. Now I don't—mind dying. Only way out—Fox." Her attempted smile was a bloody grimace.

"Where'd the bastard go?" Edley asked hoarsely.

"Downtown—I s'pose. Going to arrest—Ashley and crew—when they bring—herd in."

"I'll send the best doctor. And someone for the kids, Sue."

"Forget the doctor. Just look—after the kids. Hand me that—pad and pencil—on the table. Started to write —it all out. Got to finish—while I got—strength."

Fox Edley gave her the notepad and pencil. "Where's the sonofabitch hide out? We never found the place." He stood up and shucked his gunbelt into position, face a bone-bleak mask.

"He's always—in city hall." Her voice was getting weaker.

"*City hall?* Cano don't hang around city hall, for chrisake."

It was Susan's turn to show amazement. "It's not Hook Cano. . . . It's Milo Bascomb. . . . Thought you knew—everyone knew. . . . Hook and his men—run errands—for Milo Bascomb."

"Sweet jeezus christ!" gasped Fox Edley. "The judge himself." He laughed wildly. "Well, he'll be easier to burn down than Cano."

Susan moved her head on the pillows. "No, no, you're wrong, Fox!" She spoke with urgent force. "Milo's good—with a gun. Watch yourself."

"He ain't that good," Edley gritted, yellow eyes flaring in his scarred brown features. "I'll smoke the goddamn hypocrite!" His snarl turned quickly into a crooked smile. "Hang on, Susan. I'll send help right away."

"Goodbye, Foxcroft." Her tortured gray eyes welled with tears, as she watched him go. Then, setting her teeth, she returned to scribbling on the white pad, desperate to inform the world that her husband was no suicide, and she and Milo Bascomb were his murderers. Before she died.

Outside the house, Fox Edley grabbed up the reins, made a flying mount, and drove the blue roan like mad for the center of town, ripping down the dark streets like a man berserk on a runaway bronco.

A single thought blazed at white heat in the Fox's brain. He must find and kill Judge Milo Bascomb. Nothing else mattered at the moment.

He rocketed past three riders and a packhorse, scarcely noticing the tall man and two women coming upgrade in the opposite direction, but they halted and turned to gaze after him. "Drunk or crazy," commented Donna Ashley.

"That was Fox Edley," said Rammel. "His eyes shone like that big cat's up in the Sacramentos. There's going to be mayhem wherever the Fox lands. We better go after him, ladies."

"Why not?" Melissa Johnson said. "I missed all the action on the trail."

Wheeling their mounts around they followed the streamers of dust down the hillside toward the lights of the central plaza. Hitting the north end of El Paso, they'd decided to stop first at Rube Caldwell's home, but the hell-for-leather passing of Fox Edley changed their minds. Something urgent must have set Fox off into that wild flight, and Rammel wanted to see how and where it terminated. From the look of Fox, someone was slated to die.

Reaching the plaza at a gallop, Fox flung himself from the saddle at the hitchrack before the mud-brick hulk of city hall, paying no heed to the massed people in front of the nearby jailhouse. He went in like a one-man army of vengeance, flicking his Ranger star at the blue-clad sentries on the main entrance. He took the stairs three at a time, and the pair of guards at the top had decided to let him by, even before they saw the badge in his palm. A glance at his burning yellow eyes and hard-boned countenance was sufficient.

Fox Edley burst into the mayor's office, and Amos Essling cowered behind his desk. On his right, Fribance and Yaeger went rigid in their chairs. Judge Milo Bascomb, at the mayor's left, was the only one who rose to meet the intruder, impeccably clothed as usual, cool and serene.

"What do you want here, Ranger?" asked Bascomb.

"I want you," Fox Edley said. "I'm charging you with murder."

Bascomb laughed scornfully. "You must be joking or out of your mind. What kind of a gag is this? Murder? That's absurd."

"No joke. You comin peaceful, or you want it the hard way?"

"I happen to be the judge of El Paso County."

"I don't care a goddamn if you're attorney general of the United States," Edley said. "You're a murderer and I'm puttin you away."

Bascomb unbuttoned his brown suitcoat and stood with arms akimbo. "Whom am I supposed to have killed?" His narrowed eyes flicked to Yeager and

Fribance, who stirred tensely in their chairs. "Who are my victims?"

"You killed Rube Caldwell, and prob'ly three other Rangers. You killed Susan Caldwell tonight. You ordered the murder of Lily Lavoy, and God knows how many others. That's just a few of your crimes."

"You're insane, man," Bascomb said calmly. "A stark raving maniac."

Fribance and Yeager got to their feet, brushing coattails back to clear their pistols. When the judge drew, they would shoot Edley from the side. Nothing could be easier. Their gloating smirks vanished as the door opened and Aubrey Rammel walked in, lithe and graceful, his green stare fixed on them.

"You two boys stay out of it," Ram drawled. "This is between the judge and Foxcroft."

"Howdy, Ram," said Edley, without glancing around, his amber eyes staying on the handsome Bascomb. "What's it goin to be, Judge? An arrest or a shootout? They say you're sneaky quick with a sixgun."

"This is ridiculous," Bascomb declared. "You have no evidence, no grounds, nothing. Mayor, order these—these madmen out of your office."

Essling whooshed through his lips, but only a spray of spittle emerged. Rammel hadn't touched his Colt, yet the councilmen felt they were already covered. Bascomb's look was a command, but they could not move.

"I got a signed statement from Susan Caldwell—before she died," Fox Edley said. "You're one dead sonofabitch."

Bascomb's elegant facade was crumbling, but he reached for his belt with the snarl of a cornered animal. Fox Edley, scarcely seeming to stir, was far ahead of him, .44 aflame, drilling the judge low in the abdomen. Bent double, Bascomb fired into the floor, raising a gout of splinters, and reeled back on stuttering legs to collapse into a purple leather chair.

Frantically he fought to control his gunhand, but his second bullet flew high, smashed a crystal chandelier, and sprayed glittering glass fragments over the room. Fox Edley shot him in the chest, then the throat, the explosions melding into one blast. Chair and man both went over, Bascomb's head unhinged and blood spurting as he rolled disjointedly and lay sprawled face-down in a scarlet pool.

The hands of Yeager and Fribance twitched, but came to a trembling stop. Even yet Rammel hadn't drawn. With a boyish grin, he said, "Go ahead, try it. Let's have some more fireworks here."

They exchanged glances, wagged their heads, and let their hands fall loosely.

Fox Edley switched his gun onto the horrified mayor. "Did they arrest the Ashley crew? Get on the phone, tell 'em to let 'em go. Move, you fat bastard!"

Essling called the jail and, voice quavering, ordered the release of the Anvil prisoners. "What d'yuh mean they're already out?" he screamed. "Where's Drumm, for jeezus' sake? What say? *What?* Oh, to hell with it."

Fox Edley smiled thinly. "Now we'll go over there and put you three polecats in them cells." He turned the Colt on Yeager and Fribance. "Drop them guns." They did, and he wheeled back to Essling. "You packin iron, Mayor? No, I reckon not. All right, let's move out."

"Drumm'll kill you!" cried Essling.

Edley chortled. "I got an idea Lash and Red Bush have already took care of Drumm. Come on, sashay along, you political pricks."

Edley and Rammel shook hands as they herded the trio toward the door.

"You didn't even draw, Ram." Broken glass crunched under their boots.

"Didn't need to, Fox."

"You better pull one now," Edley said. "They got guards out there."

Rammel flipped out a .44. "They won't bother us, Foxcroft."

He was right, they didn't. They let the procession pass without a word or move of protest.

"The judge won't be holding court tomorrow," Rammel told one of the upstairs policemen. "You boys ought to take him to the morgue or the undertaker."

The guards grinned as if not displeased in the least, looking at the mayor and his aides with loathing.

Downstairs one of the outside cops asked, "What the hell's goin on anyway?"

"Law and order have returned to your fair city," Rammel said.

"It's about time, for chrisake," said the other sentry. "We heard Hook Cano and Tatum went down tonight. Across the river in *El Conquistador*. Lashtrow and Bouchard shot the shit outa them." He peered closer at Edley. "I guess you know, Fox, what happened to Fasaro last night."

"They was just errand boys for Judge Bascomb," said Fox Edley. "Where's the nearest telephone?" He received directions and hastened off, with a parting word for Rammel, "Deposit them three prize assholes in the calaboose, Ram."

"Yas *suh,* boss," Rammel tossed back at him.

The policemen wanted to escort the captives across the street, and Rammel had no objection.

"They say Bouchard's shaved off his beard," remarked the big cop.

"Holy jeezus," Rammel murmured in awed tones. "I can't wait to see that. Always wanted to see what Red

205

Bush looked like under those whiskers."

"I guess he ain't too pretty," the short cop said. "But he's sure one helluva man!"

"That he is, for certain."

"How about that Lashtrow? Ain't he somethin though?"

"He isn't bad," Ram said. "In fact you might say he's the best."

"Reckon all you Rangers are plenty goddamn good."

"Yeah, we have to be," Rammel agreed, with a modest smile. "To uphold the high traditions of Jack Hays and Big Foot Wallace, Tonk Hiller, Anse Amidon, Cactus Bill McKenna, and all the great ones."

Fox Edley overtook them on the opposite sidewalk, where the crowd was diminishing. Hoarse shouts went up as Essling, Fribance, and Yeager were recognized as prisoners. "Lynch 'em, string 'em up, hang the sonsabitches!" a man yelled over the general uproar. News spread like a prairie fire in these border towns. Rammel smiled and waved nonchalantly to Donna Ashley and Melissa Johnson on the fringe of the assemblage.

Inside the jail, Lashtrow, Bouchard, and an irate group of deputized citizens had already taken charge, freeing Ashley and his crew, throwing Sheriff Drumm and his top deputies into cells. Drumm sat on the wooden bunk in his iron-barred cage, head in hands. He looked up at this fresh influx, revealing blackened eyes, a broken bleeding nose, welted jawbones, and a swollen, lacerated mouth.

Lash got in close enough so he didn't have to use a gun, Rammel thought. But the big guy ought to be more careful of his hands.

Mayor Essling and his two councilmen were unceremoniously shoved into a cell of their own.

Ashley inquired anxiously for his daughter, and

rushed to the door when Ram told him she was outside. Arizona, Cobb and Val Verde plowed after him.

Milton Travers was there too, rather pale and stiff in a chair, his left side heavily bandaged, a bottle of brandy in his right hand. He rose with deliberate care to join Lashtrow in welcoming Rammel back to the ranks, and learn what had occurred in city hall.

"Where's Judge Bascomb?" asked Lashtrow.

"Dead as hell," Rammel drawled. "The Fox shot him in the mayor's office. Foxcroft looked very good indeed."

Fox Edley moved into the small group. "Bascomb murdered Rube Caldwell—with Susan's help. She told me tonight—after the judge stabbed her. She was writin a death-bed statement. Bascomb was her man all along, and the real head of the outlaws. He used Hook Cano and his outfit for hired killers and errand boys. All the city officials were in on it. Goin to be one christ-awful mess to clear up."

The listening men shook their heads and swore softly, almost unable to assimilate the shocking news.

"Well, I've already wired for U.S. Marshals and government lawyers," Lashtrow said. "Knew it was going to be more than we could handle, once we cleaned out city hall. The goddamn litigation will go on for months and months, maybe years."

Rusty Bouchard had joined them. "It'll clear Rube Caldwell's name of suicide anyway. Never did believe Rube coulda killed himself."

Fox Edley and Rammel gazed in disbelief at Bouchard's clean-shaven battered face.

"Christ at the crossroads!" murmured Edley. "No wonder you wore that goddamn beard all them years, Red Bush! It's your bounden duty to hide a mug like that from the public."

"Figgered shavin it'd disguise me in Juarez," said

Bouchard, unabashed. "Didn't work worth a damn. They had me nailed to the wall, till Lash blew in. I'm lettin it grow back fast as I can, Foxhead."

"Aw, it ain't that bad, Rusty." Fox smiled gently at him. "I was just horsin yuh round a little."

"I know that, for chrisake. You wouldn't dare to insult me in a serious way, you broken-down bronc-peeler."

"You look fine to me, Red Bush," said Rammel. "It's a face with character, dignity, and strength."

"Sure, I know that too, Ram." Bouchard laughed merrily. "But I feel better with the beard on."

Travers drank thoughtfully from the bottle. "I'm about ready to resign, I think. Too many slugs hitting me lately. Tends to make me believe my number's coming up soon."

"You can't get out until this case is settled, Trav," said Lashtrow, with heartless satisfaction. "You're a material witness, Milton the Third."

Travers smiled sadly. "This goddamn case'll last long enough to get us all killed, no doubt."

Bouchard gulped brandy from Trav's bottle, clapped him on the shoulder, and started to sing in a rough rollicking voice:

"Oh pray for the Ranger, you kind-hearted stranger,
He has roamed the prairies for many a year;
He has kept the Comanches from off of your ranches,
And guarded your homes o'er the far frontier."

EPILOGUE

All week in the twin border towns on the Rio Grande, mission and church bells tolled for the dead. The *bandidos*—Cano, Fasaro, Pablito, and Tatum—were buried with pomp and ceremony in Juarez, still heroes to much of the Mexican population. In El Paso, simple private services were held for Susan Caldwell and Milo Bascomb, their guilt and shame exposed for the first time.

United States Marshals and teams of lawyers arrived to assume control of the town and county government. More officials were arrested, pending in-depth investigations. Like Essling, Fribance, and Yeager, they were held without bail. Milo Bascomb's overly rich bank account was confiscated.

The Rangers, although they had become living legends, were forced to spend long boring hours and days in conference with the federal agents. Captain Bill McKenna came up from Austin to take some of the burden off their backs. Everywhere they appeared men wanted to shake their hands and buy them drinks.

The Ashley family enjoyed a happy reunion and, at

the Rangers' request, moved into the Caldwell home, so Amanda and Donna could care for the three children. Melissa Johnson entered the hospital to complete her cure for drug addiction.

Huffnail and Millhauser did not show up to purchase the Anvil herd. It remained in the stockyards, with Cobb, Arizona and Val Verde staying nearby in the Hotel Pueblo to keep watch of the cattle.

Ashley had to borrow money to pay off his Mexican helpers and send them home. Also to bring the wages of his regular cowboys up to date. Milt Travers cheerfully donated the funds for this.

The El Paso *Times* devoted nearly an entire issue to eulogizing Rube Caldwell as an immortal hero of the Texas Rangers.

Lashtrow wrote to Karen Lindley in San Antone, and learned by return mail from Ma Lindley that Karen was visiting Tess Hiller Rammel in Austin. "I'm glad she isn't pining away," Lash remarked.

Travers telegraphed Priscilla Cabot in Boston, and was informed by wire that she had embarked on a cruise to Europe with a party of friends. "That ought to tell me something," Trav observed dryly.

Down in Galeana, Chappy Chiapas caught his niece Rosita Shaw in bed with a Mex sheepherder. Chappy gave her a touch of the quirt, and enough *dinero* to get back to El Paso, where she promptly started hunting for Arizona and/or Milt Travers. Eventually she caught up with Arizona in Ben Dowell's famous saloon.

Donna Ashley had been as diligent in seeking out Rammel, but Ram had become hard to find.

When the news of the Ranger triumph reached Pinon, New Mexico, Marshal Monk Moncrief, Barber Joe Drury, and Doc Ward Bailey got together in the doctor's study to celebrate and drink countless toasts to Aubrey Rammel and the Ashley family.

Susan Caldwell's dying note, which incriminated Bascomb and herself, named Edley and Lashtrow administrators of the estate, which Rube had willed to her, with the children's money held in trust until they became of age. The original will had left his black stallion to Edley, and an unused ranch to Lash.

In consultation with the Ashleys in the Caldwell living room, Lashtrow said: "Owning property makes me uncomfortable, specially when I have no use for it. I'm not ready yet to quit the Rangers and settle down to ranching. I'm not sure that I ever will be. Now that ranch out there's going to waste, and it's a shame. The big house, bunkhouse, barns, sheds, corrals are in good shape, begging to be used. There's water and grass in plenty. No reason, Ash, why you shouldn't move in and run your stock there."

The long, gaunt-faced Ashley shook his narrow head, deep-set eyes sorrowful, leathery cheeks seamed. "My God, Lash, you've done more than enough for us already. We can't accept any more from you. That spread's worth a lotta money.

"Didn't cost me a cent. I don't feel it's really mine. You've got to use it, Ash."

"We'll pay rent then, till we can buy."

Lashtrow shrugged. "It'll go to the estate, for the kids. Either from me or straight from you." He smiled his slow gentle smile. "There's one catch, Ash. The Caldwell kids go with the ranch."

"You call that a catch?" Ashley grinned, his set features relaxing.

"I've always wanted more children," Amanda said, brightening. "We only had one that lived to grow up, Lash. I'm young enough to raise another family, and I love these little ones."

"Best place I know of for kids to grow up," Lashtrow drawled. "On a ranch with folks like you."

"Donna and I'll teach them all the lessons," Amanda said eagerly. "Donna's good at that, a born teacher."

The girl nodded and smiled faintly. Donna liked the children, but her thoughts were on Rammel.

"All right, Lash. We'll take it—on a temporary basis." Ashley was squeezing his eyelids to restrain the tears.

"It's yours as long as you want it," Lashtrow told him, as the three Anvil cowboys came in brandishing bottles and laughing.

"Compliments a Ben Dowell," said Arizona. "Won a shootin match with him in his backyard. Three bottles a the best in the house."

"*I* won the match," Val Verde declared dourly. "Tell it like it was, loudmouth."

Ashley was grateful when big Cobb shoved a bottle into his hand, and little Val Verde yanked the cork out. Ash took a good long swig, and let the moisture overflow his eyes and trickle down his thin, weathered cheeks.

That firewater was powerful enough to bring tears to the eyes of any strong man. Ashley wouldn't have to conceal the fact that he was crying a little.

Arizona was pouring delicately for the ladies, and adding water from the *olla*. "We ain't really celebrated yet, folks. Let's all get a mite drunk, amigos."

"That's the ticket, kid," said Lashtrow, with his slow, wide smile.

"I think Ram and the others should be here." Donna's hazel eyes dropped shyly to the glass in her hand.

"They will be, honey," Arizona promised gaily. "Soon as they finish playin that big poolgame downtown."

Winners of the SPUR and WESTERN HERITAGE AWARD

Awarded annually by the Western Writers of America, the Golden Spur is the most prestigious prize a Western novel, or author, can attain.

J. R. ROBERTS

THE GUNSMITH

SERIES

An all new series of adult westerns, following the wild and lusty adventures of Clint Adams, the Gunsmith!